Kyle searched her face before reluctantly releasing her arm. "Sell the land to me and it will no longer be an issue between us, Becky," he urged with rough gentleness. "When the deal is concluded, you'll see that our relationship is independent of it. I'll still want you as badly as I do now. Nothing will change between us."

She couldn't help but marvel at the sheer scope of his nerve. "You don't ask much, do you?"

"Just your trust."

"And what do I get out of it?"

He frowned. "Everything you've had until now. Our relationship will return to the way it was until this morning."

"I hate to tell you this, Kyle, but I'm afraid things can never go back to the way they were between us. Too much has happened. I want more than you can give."

"A master of the genre...nobody does it better!"
—*Romantic Times*

Jayne Ann Krentz

A Woman's Touch

MIRA

MIRA

ISBN 1-55166-315-5

A WOMAN'S TOUCH

Copyright © 1989 by Jayne Ann Krentz.

All rights reserved. Except for use in any review, the reproduction or
utilization of this work in whole or in part in any form by any electronic,
mechanical or other means, now known or hereafter invented, including
xerography, photocopying and recording, or in any information storage or
retrieval system, is forbidden without the written permission of the publisher,
MIRA Books, 225 Duncan Mill Road, Don Mills, Ontario, Canada M3B 3K9.

All characters in this book have no existence outside the imagination of the
author and have no relation whatsoever to anyone bearing the same name
or names. They are not even distantly inspired by any individual known or
unknown to the author, and all incidents are pure invention.

MIRA and the star colophon are registered trademarks of MIRA Books.

Printed in U.S.A.

A
Woman's
Touch

PROLOGUE

From the journal of Alice Cork

I sold the milk cow today. Won't be needing her any-more. Let her go real cheap to the Mintons. They'll take good care of her. They lost their cow last winter and Lord knows they could use the milk. There's another little one on the way. Told Abby Minton to make ar-rangements with the doctor in town because this time I don't think I'll be here when the baby arrives. She didn't want to believe me, but I know it's true. Got feel-ings about it. I won't be seeing another winter in this valley.

The cow was the last of the stock. Everything else is taken care of. Talked to that Denver lawyer yesterday. He says he'll handle things just the way I told him right down to publishing the contents of my will in the local paper.

Harmony Valley is safe. Kyle Stockbridge and Glen Ballard will explode when they find out the land is go-ing to distant kin of mine, but there isn't a damned thing they can do about it. Reckon it's all the vengeance I'm going to get.

I wonder what this Rebecca Wade is like. Feels strange to be leaving the land to someone I've never even met. But I've got a feeling about her. I've had it for months—ever since I came across her name when I was putting together the family tree last year. It's the same kind of feeling I get when I know there's a storm coming or when one of the local women is expecting a baby. I just sort of know Rebecca's the right one.

If there was more time I'd try to find her and warn her about what she's going to be up against. But I'm just plumb worn out. Don't have the strength or the time left to look her up. I'll leave that to the lawyer to do after I'm gone. Lord knows I'm paying him enough.

But Rebecca Wade, whoever she is, is sure going to have her hands full dealing with Stockbridge and Ballard. A fire-breathing dragon and a slick-talking sorcerer. They won't make it easy on her. Something tells me Rebecca is going to be the one to handle them, though.

There was a time back when I was a lot younger when I would have sworn there was no hope for any male born a Stockbridge or a Ballard. I'd have said they were all doomed to be out-and-out bastards right from the start. But now I'm not so sure. Kyle and Glen, whether they know it or not, aren't mirror images of their fathers or their grandfathers. The right woman might be able to change everything around here.

ONE

The sweeping tide of desire that surged through him was strong enough to make him shudder. It clawed at his insides and made him dangerously restless. When he had begun the search for Rebecca, he'd never anticipated this. Two months ago when he had found her, he'd been sure everything was under control. He'd been pleased with the coup. His luck was holding, he'd told himself.

But he had wanted her violently on sight and the past two months had been torture. At first he'd told himself he could handle it. But something had gone wrong somewhere along the line. He couldn't even pinpoint the exact moment when the situation had started to turn impossible. All he knew was that tonight he was overwhelmed with a devastating passion he could no longer ignore.

Kyle Stockbridge acknowledged at last that he'd been caught in his own trap.

Until this moment he had been the hunter—surefooted, confident, clever. But as of this instant he finally admitted he was in serious jeopardy. If he was not extremely careful, he would become the victim. And the role of victim was one Kyle Stockbridge never played.

He stared at the woman with the amber eyes, watching her as she chatted with friends and co-workers on the other side of the crowded room. Voices hummed around him. Ice clinked in glasses. The strains of background music provided by a small trio filled the air. Stockbridge tuned out everything except the sight of Rebecca Wade.

He still felt like a predator, filled with an insatiable hunger. But that hunger made him vulnerable, he told himself. He would have to be more cautious than ever.

For two months he'd been playing a reckless game with a woman who excited him as no other woman ever had. Rebecca was not a stunningly beautiful female. She was no exotic, bewitching siren who lured men with some strange, captivating magic.

She was simply Rebecca, and she worked for him. She had only been at Flaming Luck Enterprises for two months but already she had left an indelible mark on the place.

Awesomely organized, efficient and intelligent, Rebecca had turned the place upside down. She had a flair for management. As Kyle's executive assistant she had restructured everything from his daily routine to the way the mail clerk delivered the mail.

Most importantly, as far as his staff was concerned, Rebecca could handle the boss. Kyle's temper was legendary, but he never lost his temper with Rebecca. *Never.*

True—he argued with her frequently, occasionally growled impatiently when he was dissatisfied, and sometimes he snapped when she overstepped even the wide bounds he had indulgently allowed her. But he never really lost his temper. Not the way he did with lesser mortals.

They called her the Lady with the Magic Wand, Kyle knew. The image amused him, but there was an element of truth in it. When he was breathing fire and no one else dared enter his office, Rebecca could walk calmly into the dragon's lair and emerge unruffled and unscathed.

He had wondered just what he had let himself in for at the end of her first week of employment. She had breezed into his office, omnipresent clipboard in hand, and announced that she was instituting a series of weekly reports. These Friday morning reports were to be viewed as a management tool, she'd informed him.

"Your management techniques are barbaric," she'd stated. "I'll grant that your blunt way of doing business attracts and holds a certain type of client who appreciates directness and honesty. But dealing with one's employees requires a slightly different approach."

"I'm not supposed to be honest with my employees?"

"You are supposed to be *diplomatic* with your staff."

"Diplomacy, Miss Wade, is not one of my strong points."

"Then you'll have to work on that element of your management style, won't you, Mr. Stockbridge?" she had retorted with a charming smile. "And while you're at it, you'll start working on other management techniques, too. It's time, Mr. Stockbridge, that you learned to delegate."

"I like to know what my people are doing." He'd defended himself with a scowl.

"There are other ways of finding out besides looking over their shoulders." She'd frowned slightly in concentration as she'd bent over her clipboard. "Now, then, the first item on this week's report is…"

"My name."

She'd looked up quizzically. "I beg your pardon?"

"The first item on the weekly report is my name. If you're going to take over my company, Rebecca, we might as well put ourselves on a first-name basis."

She'd been slightly flustered. "I assure you, I have no intention of usurping your authority, Mr. Stockbridge."

"Then try to follow a few of my orders from time to time. It will create the illusion that I'm still in charge. Call me Kyle."

She'd smiled slowly, a little shyly. "Very well, Kyle."

That smile had done dangerous things to his insides. He'd sat and watched as she'd returned to the weekly report, and all he'd been able to think about was what it would be like to remove her neat, professional little black-and-white checked suit and lay her down on the leather couch in the corner. He'd had a feeling Rebecca Wade's creamy body would look very good lying nude on rich cordovan brown leather.

In the following days she had set about changing the way he functioned in his own office. For the first time in his life, Kyle was learning what it meant to delegate authority. He wasn't sure he liked running his business that way, but so far things seemed to be working.

She was attractive enough, Kyle told himself, striving to be objective, but definitely not outstanding. There were other women in the room who were far more beautiful although he discovered he couldn't seem to name one right offhand.

Rebecca's rich, dark brown hair was sleek and shining tonight, he noted. She had it in a classic twist that exposed her delicate ears and the small gold rings she wore in them. The style also revealed her nape, which for some reason seemed incredibly sexy to Kyle. He had a violent urge to stroke her there where he knew she would be soft and sensitive and very, very vulnerable.

Taken individually, the rest of Rebecca's features were unremarkable, with the exception of her spectacular amber eyes. A straight, no-nonsense nose, a firm little chin, a mouth that smiled readily—all pleasant enough, but not stunning. But the whole was animated by an intelligent awareness and an interest in others that made anyone who talked to her, even in passing, feel special. Men and women alike preened and glowed under the impact of that genuine interest.

She stood somewhere around five-foot-five or five-foot-six, although the impossibly high heels she wore tonight gave an illusion of added height. The rose-colored, drop-waisted silk dress she had on skimmed her slender figure, hinting at the small, high breasts and nicely rounded hips.

Kyle was thinking about the subtle, feminine strength in that slender body when he noticed a familiar figure in a dark Italian-cut jacket move in on Rebecca. Broad male shoulders cut her off from Kyle's sight. He saw the smile of welcome on her lips as she turned to greet the newcomer, and a shaft of pure, primitive possessiveness knifed through him. Instinctively he started through the crowd to stake his claim.

He knew then with absolute certainty that he had to take her to bed tonight. He had to end the torment he had unwittingly inflicted on himself for the past two months. It was the only way he would find any peace now. Afterward he would tell her everything.

There would be time enough to tell her the whole truth after he'd made love to her. She'd understand. She *had* to understand. He would make sure of that.

Rebecca saw Kyle moving toward her. Out of

the corner of her eye she watched him cut through the crowded room. He moved with the arrogant assurance of a nineteenth-century western gunslinger walking through a saloon full of gamblers and rowdies. No one got in his way for long, she noticed. Rebecca hid a smile as he reached her side.

"Hello, Harrison," Kyle said. There was enough of an edge on his low growl of a voice to make the other man blink. There was also a strong hint of the western drawl that only emerged when Kyle was annoyed. "I didn't know you were going to be here tonight. Thought you went out of your way to avoid these things."

Rick Harrison, a young, up-and-coming member of the marketing department of Flaming Luck Enterprises eyed his boss with due caution. Then he smiled at Rebecca. "Becky talked me into doing my duty tonight. She says I ought to mingle more with the clients. She also gave me her word she'd made certain Flaming Luck was using a new caterer for its corporate entertaining these days. I think I was poisoned last time."

"Since you're here for the food, why don't you give the buffet table a try?" Kyle suggested meaningfully. "It sure as hell is costing me enough, though, so leave something for the clients. Looks like every damned one of them turned up tonight. Nothing like free food and booze to bring 'em out of the woodwork."

Rick's brows rose at the obvious dismissal. He gave Rebecca a knowing grin. "I see he hasn't stopped complaining about the tab for this little extravaganza."

Rebecca laughed. "He's been screaming for a month. You'd think I'd hired a four-star chef and served nothing but caviar and champagne. I'm sure I'll get lectures on unnecessary corporate extravagance until the next Flaming Luck anniversary party. Then he can start grumbling all over again."

"Be glad you're not married to the man," Rick murmured quite audibly as he turned away. "You'd probably have to account for every little charge-card expense."

Rebecca felt herself turning pink. The thought of anything permanent with Kyle, let alone the thought of marriage, was enough to set off a wave of longing and excitement deep within her. She tried to suppress the heady emotions, deliberately avoiding Kyle's too-observant gaze as she took a discreet sip of the drink in her hand.

It was Kyle who broke the tiny, taut silence that followed in the wake of Rick's parting remark. "I never scream," he said mildly. His green eyes were gleaming.

Rebecca gave that some thought. "*Roar* might be a better description."

"Lately people have been depending on you to pacify me when I feel like roaring. Didn't take them long, did it? You've only been working as my executive assistant for two months, and already everyone from my secretary to the janitor counts on you to keep me happy and content.

You've been elected chief soother of the savage beast.''

"That's nonsense.''

Kyle shrugged and took a swallow of his whiskey. "No, it's not. I've seen the way people check with you first to find out what kind of mood I'm in before they come into my office. And don't think I haven't realized that the more fainthearted types have started asking you to run interference for them, so they won't have to face me themselves when things go wrong.''

Rebecca frowned. That last comment was very close to the truth. She'd been asked on more than one occasion to brave her boss's temper on behalf of some nervous midlevel manager.

"I don't know why everyone thinks I've got some sort of special touch when it comes to dealing with you. The truth is, you do tend to scream—excuse me, I mean roar—occasionally, but in the end you're generally quite reasonable.''

Kyle gave her a look that was halfway between astonishment and amusement. "There are people in this room tonight who would collapse laughing if they heard you say that.''

"Why?'' she demanded. Lately she had begun to feel as if there were a joke going around. One for which everyone at Flaming Luck, except her, knew the punch line.

"Let's just say I've got a reputation for being difficult.''

"Most men in your position are occasionally difficult,'' Rebecca said philosophically. "Not that being the boss excuses your rudeness and inconsiderate behavior, of course," she added firmly.

"I'll keep that in mind. I do appreciate the lecture on manners, ma'am." Kyle's hard mouth was edged with faint mockery.

Rebecca hesitated and then took the plunge. She had to know. "Well?" she challenged softly.

Kyle looked at her. "Well, what?"

"Why do people think I've got some sort of magic touch with you? Were you really all that difficult to deal with before I joined Flaming Luck?"

Kyle contemplated that for a moment. "Richardson in personnel has a diplomatic way of explaining it. He says you've brought a touch of civilization to Flaming Luck."

Rebecca smiled slowly, feeling a warm glow. "That's nice to hear. Not the usual sort of personnel evaluation, but rather charming. I hope he remembers to jot that down in my file."

"Some of the others have a less diplomatic way of explaining your magic touch," Kyle went on very gently.

Rebecca's smile faded. She met his gaze, her own full of sudden wariness. "What do some of the others say?"

"They say the reason you can wrap me around your little finger so easily is that you're sleeping with me."

Rebecca nearly dropped her wineglass. For an instant she couldn't think at all. Shock ripped through her. It was as if Kyle had read her mind and viewed her secret fantasies. Kyle and everyone else on his staff, apparently. She struggled to regain her self-control.

"No," she whispered, dazed at the implications. If people were really saying such things, she was in a terrible mess. She would have no choice but to leave Flaming Luck Enterprises. "*No*," she said again, agonized. "Why would anyone say such a thing? We haven't...I mean we aren't even dating, let alone sleeping together. I don't understand. It's not right. They can't say such things. There's no basis for it. Our relationship has been totally professional. How dare anyone imply...?" She broke off, floundering.

Kyle's watchful eyes narrowed as he studied the stunned expression on her face. "Would it be so bad?" he asked with typical bluntness.

"How can you say that? It would be terrible. That kind of gossip is destructive and dangerous." Rebecca was beginning to feel frantic. "It has to be stopped."

"Why?"

"Because it's not true," she said desperately. "What's the matter with you? Don't you understand?"

"I've got news for you, Becky. People have affairs all the time in the workplace these days."

"I don't!"

He smiled grimly. "No, you don't, do you? You've got a downright prudish notion of proper office behavior. Your old boss told me all about how *professional* you always were. He said you wouldn't even date anyone you worked with. And I've seen the way you handle the male half of my staff. But there's a first time for everything. Answer my question. Would sleeping with me be all that bad?"

"For heaven's sake, how can you ask me such a thing?"

"Think about it."

"*Kyle*."

He ignored her, his gaze on a portly man across the room. "I just saw Clifton Peabody come in. Considering all the money we made off him last year, I'd better say hello to him. Excuse me, Becky. I'll be back in a few minutes." He started off and then halted and swung around at the last minute. "Harrison was wrong, you know."

Rebecca was too shaken to comprehend. "Wrong about what?"

"If you came to live with me, I wouldn't scream about every entry on the charge-card bills. I would be generous with you, Becky."

Rebecca was suddenly incensed. Pure, clean anger burned away the confusion and near hysteria she had been experiencing. "I have my own charge cards," she said through her teeth. "I don't need to use yours or anyone else's."

But she couldn't be sure he had heard her. Kyle had already turned away to slice back into the crowd. Rebecca stared after his departing figure. She felt light-headed. In her wildest fantasies she'd never imagined the kind of conversation she'd just had with Kyle Stockbridge.

The fact that they had just skated along the surface of her most secret dreams was unnerving enough. Having Kyle practically tell her he wouldn't mind becoming romantically involved with her was shattering. Reality that came too close to fantasy had to be dangerous.

Harrison was wrong. If you came to live with me…

Rick Harrison had said something about marriage, not about living together, Rebecca reminded herself stoutly. Kyle had conveniently dropped the word "marriage" when he had referred to Rick's teasing comment.

But, then, Kyle was feeling his way, Rebecca realized suddenly. He was being cautious. After all, he had just opened up the subject they'd both been assiduously avoiding for the past two months. Tonight was the first time either of them had actually confronted, even obliquely, the matter of their mutual attraction.

Thank goodness it was mutual, Rebecca found herself thinking with a curious relief. Apparently Kyle had been as aware of the energy between them as she had. It hadn't been just a figment of her imagination after all. Until now she hadn't been certain that he'd wanted her as much as she wanted him.

The dangerous part was that she was not just attracted to Kyle. Rebecca was very much afraid she was in love with the man. She had a hunch she was asking for trouble with a capital *T*.

In spite of the well-cut suits and crisp white shirts he favored, Kyle Stockbridge frequently reminded her of some legendary male straight out of the Old West. Self-contained, arrogant, aggressive and frequently unreadable. He should have been born a hundred years ago when cowboys, desperadoes, gamblers and gunmen roamed this part of Colorado. He would have been right at home.

Not that he didn't fit in well with the modern Denver, Rebecca admitted to herself. He moved very successfully in its business circles. During the two months she'd worked for him, she'd seen just how skillfully he played the high-stakes games corporations play.

Flaming Luck Enterprises was a thriving firm involved in commercial real-estate development. The company had a reputation for being in the right place at the right time—a reputation for luck.

But no matter how many modern business coups he pulled off, Rebecca knew she would always see Kyle as something of an anomaly. He had a tough, old-fashioned machismo about him that didn't quite jibe with contemporary sensitivities. He should have owned a black stallion, not a black Porsche. He ought to be wearing leather and denim, not a business suit. And he would have looked as comfortable carrying a Colt Single Action revolver as he did carrying a briefcase.

Kyle Stockbridge was tough-looking, not good-looking. He was iron and granite in an era of glass and chrome. His roughly carved face had the implacable quality of a Rocky Mountain peak in winter. His eyes were green, flecked with gold and he studied his environment with sharp intelligence. He was a notch or two under six feet, but there was an aura of power in his lean, taut frame.

He would make an awesome enemy, Rebecca acknowledged. But she'd known him only as a friend, a reasonably indulgent employer and as a fantasy lover. He'd been kind to her from the first, offering her a job just when the one she'd had had been about to disappear.

She'd heard about his temper but Rebecca never understood what all the fuss was about. Kyle could be irritable, demanding and difficult at times, but she'd never known him to be unfair or genuinely dangerous.

"Hi, Becky. How's it going? Looks like the fifth annual anniversary celebration of Flaming Luck Enterprises is off to a flying start. Thank heaven you convinced Stockbridge to change the caterer this year."

Rebecca turned to smile at the attractive, middle-aged woman who had just halted beside her. Natalie Penn had joined Flaming Luck's personnel department two years ago. "Hello, Natalie. I seem to be getting more comments on the food than anything else. I'm beginning to believe all those nasty rumors I heard about last year's caterers were true."

"Every last one of them was true. The buffet table was filled with limp, squishy things on wet toast. We never could identify half the stuff. Just as well, probably. But this year everything looks first-class." She glanced around the room, nodding with satisfaction. "About time Stockbridge paid some attention to this side of the business."

"I gather he's been busy with the basics for the past five years," Rebecca said quietly. "He hasn't had a lot of time to worry about polishing the image of the company. You know how he is when he's got his sights set on a particular goal. He ignores all the side issues."

"That he does." Natalie grinned. "He's good at ignoring all sorts of things that might distract him from his goal. Things like people's feelings. Things like the recommendations of his department chiefs. Things like decent caterers. Kyle Stockbridge is very, very good at going after what he wants, all right."

A small shiver traced the line of Rebecca's spine. What Natalie had said was true. Kyle could be downright single-minded. Nothing got in his way once he'd decided what he wanted. And tonight he had made it clear he wanted her.

"You make it sound as though Kyle is difficult to work for," Rebecca said quietly. "But I notice you're still with the firm after two years. With your background, you could go anywhere."

"Maybe. But I couldn't get a better salary. Believe me, I know. I checked around about a month after I took this job. Right after Stockbridge came storming into my office one morning and wanted to know where I'd been getting the turkeys I'd been sending to him to interview for a clerical position in accounting."

Rebecca shook her head in dismay. "He shouldn't have been personally interviewing candidates at that job level."

"I know, but until you came along, Stockbridge was what might charitably be called a 'hands on' administrator. He didn't trust anyone else to do anything right."

"Well, he's learning. Flaming Luck is getting too big for the boss to take a personal hand in all the small details of running an office."

"My sentiments exactly," Natalie said dryly. "But up until two months ago, we all saw and heard a bit too much of the boss. He tended to show up at the most unexpected moments. And Stockbridge can be overwhelming, even in small doses. Charm and tact are not high on his list of priorities. I'm not sure he even knows the meaning of those words."

"I'll admit he can be a little blunt at times."

"That's putting it mildly, and you know it. The man rides roughshod over anyone who gets in his way. I'll tell you truthfully, Becky, it's been nice having you to run interference lately."

Rebecca winced. "Is that the role everyone sees me in? I was hired as an executive assistant, not a...a..."

"A gladiator? Or a knight in shining armor?" Natalie chuckled. "You know something? Stockbridge never had an executive assistant until he hired you. He didn't know what to do with one. Claimed he had a secretary and that was all he needed. But two months ago he suddenly appeared in my office and told me to cut the paperwork on his first assistant. Said there wouldn't be any need to interview for the position. He'd already found the right candidate."

Rebecca shifted uneasily, a little embarrassed. "I see."

"I thought I did, too," Natalie said wryly. "I don't mind telling you I was rather skeptical of the whole situation. I couldn't figure it out. Why would Stockbridge suddenly take it into his head to hire an executive assistant who also happened to be female? Stockbridge has never allowed his private life to interfere with his business judgment. In fact, I don't think he has much in the way of a private life. He's no ladies' man, that's for sure. He practically lives at the office."

Rebecca was deeply chagrined. "You thought he'd created the position for me because of a personal relationship?"

"It did occur to me." Natalie smiled broadly. "But you've done such wonders since you arrived that I don't give a darn if you and he are having the affair of the century. And neither does anyone else. In fact, most of the staff has decided you're exactly the kind of woman he needs. He actually *listens* to you, Becky."

"I am not having an affair with him," Rebecca bit out, thoroughly exasperated now. It was worse than she had imagined. Apparently everyone thought she and Kyle were romantically involved. Now she understood the joke that she had sensed was going around. Her imaginary relationship with Kyle was apparently the punch line.

"If you say so." Natalie appeared totally unconcerned. "I guess it's not all that important as long as you have the magic touch. Just go on keeping Stockbridge off our backs and you'll have the undying gratitude of every employee at Flaming Luck. Oops, there's Richardson. I think he's trying to signal me. I'd better go see what he wants. Catch you later, Becky."

Rebecca turned in a haze and eased her way through the crowd toward a quiet corner of the room. Her head was spinning and it wasn't because of the small amount of wine she had consumed.

She could not envision a more complicated scenario if she tried. Everyone she worked with already assumed she was sleeping with the boss. Stockbridge, himself, was apparently not opposed to the idea. And as for her, she was in love with the man. A part of her desperately wanted all those rumors and assumptions to be true.

But she was thirty years old and in all the years she had been making her way in the business world, she had never once allowed herself to be involved in an office affair. She had seen the disastrous results of such alliances far too often.

A few office romances ended in marriage, but far more often they ended in uncomfortable, unpleasant, untenable situations that ultimately meant one or the other of the lovers had to quit his or her job. Business being what it was, a predominantly male-oriented world, it was usually the woman who wound up looking for work.

Rebecca had frequently vowed never to get herself into such a humiliating situation.

But she had never before fallen in love with the boss.

Nervously she surveyed the room from her sheltered corner. Kyle was on the other side, talking to another important client. Flaming Luck had recently gone after this particular client with a vengeance, Rebecca knew.

The new client had been giving a rival firm, Clear Advantage Development, his business for two years. But Kyle had set out to change the man's mind and, as usual, Kyle had gotten what he wanted.

Kyle Stockbridge was like that, Rebecca reminded herself. Once he'd made up his mind, he was unstoppable. He had enormous energy and focus. Tonight, for the first time, she'd realized he was going to turn that energy and focus on her. She had to be careful, she thought. She must be cautious.

But a part of her didn't want to be cautious. A part of her longed to surrender to the fantasy of loving Kyle.

The anniversary reception seemed to drag on forever. With an effort of will, Rebecca forced herself out of her safe little corner and mingled once more with the clients and her fellow workers. She was aware that everyone was hailing the party as a success and giving her the credit, but she couldn't seem to relax sufficiently to take much satisfaction in that success. All she could think about was what would happen when the reception ended.

Kyle was going to take her home. He had casually made the arrangements himself this afternoon. He had appeared in the doorway of her office, lounging there as if he owned the place, which, of course, he did, and told her he would pick her up after work and take her home when the reception was over.

Rebecca had not put up much resistance. She had said a polite thank-you and had given him a gracious, professional smile. Kyle had nodded brusquely and disappeared.

Now, an offer that had merely seemed polite was taking on ominous overtones. Rebecca decided against another glass of wine after she finished her first. She had a feeling she would need her wits about her later. She both anticipated and dreaded the inevitable drive home.

Shortly after ten Rebecca stood beside Kyle and watched him say goodnight to the last of his guests. In twos and threes they filed out of the hotel reception room that had been rented for the occasion and disappeared into the balmy summer evening.

When the last guest had departed, Kyle glanced around the room, which was littered with empty glasses and food trays. He nodded once in satisfaction.

"You did a good job, Becky," he said. "But I'm

glad we don't have to go through this again until next year."

"Don't forget the annual Christmas party."

"What annual Christmas party? We never have Christmas parties at Flaming Luck."

"Your reputation as Scrooge is about to undergo a change."

He groaned. "I'm not ready to face that kind of trauma yet. Wait until November before you start talking to me about a Christmas party. Ready to go?"

"I'll get my purse," she murmured and fled toward the cloakroom. The inevitable had arrived. The sensual tension between herself and Kyle was palpable. She could feel it beating at her. She heard it in his voice.

Ten minutes later he walked her out into the hotel parking lot and eased her into the cockpit of the black Porsche. Then he got in beside her and closed the door. Rebecca had a curious sensation of sliding down beneath the surface of a moonlit sea. She could still breathe here below the waves, but she felt trapped in a warm, flowing current that was carrying her toward an unseen destination.

There was silence in the Porsche as Kyle pulled out onto the street. Rebecca could feel him brooding beside her. It was not an unfamiliar experience. After working for Kyle for two months, she was becoming accustomed to his long periods of dark contemplation. She knew he was deep in his thoughts now, and she could only guess at what was going through his brain.

Was he thinking of some clever excuse for urging her to stop by his place before he drove her home? Plotting devious ways to seduce her? No, that wasn't like Kyle. He was always forthright and direct about what he wanted, often disconcertingly so. As Natalie had said, no one would ever accuse Kyle Stockbridge of being the soul of charm and tact.

She'd better think fast about just what she wanted, Rebecca decided. Kyle was something of an unknown quantity. Getting involved with him held a lot of potential risk. There were dark, heavily shadowed regions in this man, she knew—regions she might never be allowed to see our understand. She wasn't certain if she could accept a man who was so unknowable.

"You never answered my question earlier," Kyle said at last.

"Which question?" But she knew. She knew what he was going to say next. She flexed her fingers in her lap in an unconscious attempt to alleviate some of her tension.

"Would it be so hard for you to go to bed with me?"

Rebecca took a deep breath and gave in to her fantasies. "No," she whispered. "It wouldn't be hard at all."

TWO

"I'm not handling this very well. I'm sorry." Kyle's voice was low and rough as he walked over to join Rebecca in front of the vast expanse of his living-room window. He had already discarded his jacket. As he moved toward her, he tugged impatiently at the knot of his tie.

Rebecca smiled a little nervously as she surveyed the night view of Denver that was spread out before her. "Don't look at me for advice and assistance," she said, trying to keep things light. "I haven't had a lot of experience at this sort of thing, myself."

"I figured as much," he said with unexpected gentleness. "But you're my ace executive assistant. I count on you for management expertise."

"Does this kind of thing have to be *managed*?"

"We'll wing it," he promised.

Silence descended.

"I've often wondered what your home would look like," she said after a moment. "I think I expected you to have a house in the hills, not a high-rise apartment."

"This is closer to the office." He handed her one of the two glasses he'd brought with him from the kitchen.

The aroma of a potent liquor filled Rebecca's nostrils. She inhaled deeply and felt herself sinking further into the dangerous current. "And being close to the office is important to you, isn't it? Flaming Luck Enterprises is your whole life."

"Not quite. But it's sure as hell a big part of it." He was watching her profile, not the view. He hadn't bothered to turn on the living-room lights and the shadows suited him all too well. "I have a place in the mountains where I can go when I feel the need to get out of the city."

"What kind of place?" she asked curiously.

"A ranch. It's been in the family since the late eighteen hundreds. It's mine now. My father died a few years ago and left it to me."

"A working ranch?" She was suddenly, intensely interested. She could picture him on a ranch.

"Not any more. I keep a few horses for riding, but that's about it these days. In the beginning the Stockbridges ran cattle on the Flaming Luck and later there was mining. But for the past few years it's just been a place to go when I need to get away from work. Damn it, Becky, I don't want to talk about the ranch."

The glass felt warm in her hand. "What do you want to talk about?" Stupid question.

"Us. You and me." He touched the side of her face, stroking her cheek. His fingertip was a little rough, excitingly so, as if he handled leather all day instead of paper. He must have felt the small shudder that went through Rebecca. "Are you afraid of me?" he asked, his green eyes searching her face.

"No. But I am afraid of the situation," she said honestly.

He swore softly. "I know. Like I said, I'm not handling this very well. Blame it on inexperience."

Her smile was tremulous. She slanted him a quick, assessing glance. "Inexperience with office affairs, you mean?"

"I've never gotten involved with anyone who worked for me," he stated. "I've always been convinced it's a stupid thing to do."

Rebecca sighed. "It is a stupid thing to do."

"Not this time. This time, it's the only thing I can do. I have no choice. I want you, Becky. And I think you want me. I know you're nervous. I want to be able to reassure you, but I'm not certain how to go about it."

It would help if you told me you loved me, she thought. But he didn't say that. Instead, Kyle bent his head and kissed her nape. His mouth lingered there. Rebecca closed her eyes, trembling beneath the intimate caress. She turned her head and caught his hand in her fingers. She pressed her lips into his palm, aware of a wave of longing that was unlike anything she had ever known.

"*Becky.*" With a low groan Kyle reached out and took the glass from her shaking fingers. He set it down beside his own, and then he pulled her fiercely into his arms. "Nothing else matters," he muttered hoarsely. "Remember that. Whatever happens, promise me you'll remember that. This is all that's important."

She lifted her head to search his glittering green gaze for answers to unspoken questions about the past, the present and the future. But when she parted her lips to speak, Kyle took her mouth with heady aggression. A low groan of desire rumbled through his chest.

The current in which Rebecca was floating gathered force. She was no longer drifting gently toward the unseen culmination of her journey. She was being swept along on a flood tide of desire. Nothing in her past had prepared her for this level of emotional intensity. She had never expected to encounter such a violent need within herself. The depths of her own passion startled her, left her disoriented and confused. Instinctively she clung to Kyle.

Kyle's arms tightened around her, promising a haven of safety in which she could weather the approaching storm. His kiss altered, becoming less demanding and aggressive, more coaxing and intimate, probing and persuasive.

Rebecca spread her fingers across his broad shoulders, feeling the strength of him through the crisp cotton of his shirt. His muscles rippled and flexed with a promise of power and sensuality under her hands. His palms moved down her back to her waist.

"You're so slender," he said against her lips. "I feel as if I could break you in half if I wasn't careful."

Rebecca looked up at him with dreaming eyes. "Then you'll have to be very careful, won't you?"

"You have my word on it. I'll be very careful with you. Just trust me, baby. Let go of all your fears and trust me. I'll take care of everything." He lifted her up into the hard, waiting heat of his thighs, making certain she could feel the need in him.

She put her arms around his neck and kissed his throat, silently giving him her answer.

"This is going to be so good. So right." Kyle picked her up and carried her down the hall to his bedroom.

Rebecca felt the fierce determination surging in him and wondered at it. There were so many things she wanted to know in that moment, so many questions she wanted to ask. But there was no time. Kyle's urgent desire came first. She understood that because her own need was threatening to consume her. Two months of hovering on the brink of passion, eight weeks of feasting on silent fantasies were taking their toll.

Time enough to talk later, Rebecca told herself as Kyle carefully lowered her to her feet beside the wide bed in the darkened bedroom. She looked up at him.

"I love you," she whispered.

"Oh, Becky, honey," he muttered thickly. "My sweet, loyal, Becky. How did I ever get along without you?"

He covered her mouth with his own, caught her hands and guided them to the first of his shirt buttons. Her fingers shook a little as she obediently went to work to unfasten the garment. She felt his hands on the zipper of her dress.

A moment later the silk slithered softly off her shoulders and down over her hips. The dress fell in soft waves at her feet. She stepped out of her shoes, feeling intensely vulnerable. Kyle bent his head to look down at her. His eyes gleamed in the darkness.

"Tonight when I looked at you across that roomful of people, all I could think about was what you would look like without that dress on."

She saw the controlled hunger in his eyes and knew he was not disappointed. She relaxed and stepped closer, sliding her palms inside his shirt. "I suppose this is as good a time as any to tell you that I've been doing a little fantasizing of my own these past few weeks." His skin was warm, and there was a crisp mat of curling hair on his chest.

Kyle chuckled huskily. "Tell me about your fantasies and I'll tell you about mine," he urged as he began to undo the fastening of her bra.

Rebecca felt the warmth in her cheeks. "I can't tell you about them. Not yet."

"Shy? I had a hunch you would be at this stage. But that's all right. You can tell me everything later after you've had a chance to get used to my touch. In the meantime, I'll tell you what I've been thinking about all evening."

"Kyle?" She was suddenly breathless as the silky scrap of her bra fell away.

"One of the things I fantasized about was holding you like this," Kyle said softly. He cupped her gently curving breasts in his hands and ran his thumbs lightly over her nipples. "I wanted to feel your response to me. I wanted to see how full and tight you would get."

"Oh, Kyle," she moaned, closing her eyes and leaning into him. Her breasts became unbearably sensitive, her nipples taut and aching.

"You're so perfect," he whispered into her hair. "I knew it would be like this." His palms grazed her nipples again and she whimpered softly. "Am I hurting you?" he asked.

"No." She shook her head quickly. "No, it's just that I feel so sensitive, I can hardly stand it."

He smiled with a satisfaction he made no attempt to conceal. "Then I'll have to find another way to touch you there." His hands closed around her waist and he lifted her up against him.

Rebecca cried out as she felt his tongue on the throbbing peaks of her breasts. Her fingers locked onto his shoulders and her head tipped back.

"That's it, baby. You're beautiful. You're going to drive me out of my mind. That's right, sweetheart. Talk to me with those soft little sounds. Let me know how much you need me." Kyle's voice was dark and encouraging, full of praise and wonder as she trembled in his grasp.

He lowered her onto the turned-back bed, stripping off her panty hose and the small triangle of her panties in one smooth movement. Then he stood up, yanking roughly at his own clothing until the last garment was kicked aside.

Rebecca stared up at him, excitement washing over her as she took in the sight of him. Kyle's body was lean and hard, tapering from broad shoulders to narrow hips and muscular thighs. A thick nest of dark hair framed his heavy, aroused manhood.

"You're magnificent," she said, lifting one hand to touch his thigh.

"So are you. Becky, honey, we're going to be just right for each other. You'll see." He came down beside her and leaned over her, trapping her between his braced arms. "Touch me," he ordered softly. "Go ahead. Touch me. I've been driving myself crazy wondering how your hands would feel on me."

She slowly traced an intimate path with her fingertips. Her questing palms slipped down over his chest to his waist and around to the bunched muscles of his back. Rebecca stirred and moved closer to him as she became familiar with the shape and size of him.

"You feel good," she said with growing delight.

His laugh was harsh with a desire that was barely held in check. "I feel like I'm going to explode." He bent his head and kissed the valley between her breasts. "Keep going. I want your hands on me everywhere."

She knew what he was asking for, but a part of her hesitated. She'd been dreaming of this for two months but suddenly things seemed to be moving too quickly. "Kyle?"

"Everywhere." He captured one of her trailing hands and drew it down to his pulsing manhood. "Oh, yeah, baby." His western drawl was suddenly more pronounced. It gave his voice a dark, sexy sound that was as exciting as his touch. "That's what I want. Just like that. Please."

She stroked him gently, her uncertainty giving way to a thrilling excitement as she felt him respond to her. He was large and wholly male, a creature built for taking what he wanted in life. But tonight he was hers to command. He would never hurt her. But she knew he would take everything she chose to give. And she wanted to give him everything.

"That's enough," Kyle said suddenly. His hand closed around her wrist, and he pulled her fingers away from their intimate exploration. "Any more of that right now, and I won't last another minute."

Rebecca laughed up at him with silent satisfaction, glorying in her ability to make him respond so strongly to her. Her confidence was growing by leaps and bounds now. "If I'm not allowed to touch you, how are we going to pass the time?"

"I've got a few ideas on the subject." He

stroked his hand along the length of her, his palm sweeping over her breasts and down to the rounded softness of her thighs. "Open your legs for me, Becky. It's my turn to touch you."

She obeyed slowly, her sense of vulnerability increasing again. But her need to experience the full range of his lovemaking was overpowering. She turned her head into his chest and gasped as he slid his fingers into her warmth.

"You're ready for me, aren't you? Tell me you want me."

"I want you."

"You're so soft and responsive," he marveled. "So warm and wet."

She twisted sensually as he probed intimately. Her eyes squeezed shut against the wave of sensation that swept through her. Her fingers tightened on his arms as she clung to him. Her legs tangled with his and she instinctively moved her foot caressingly along his bare calf.

Kyle's reaction to her soft, seductive movements was even more violent than her own response to him. Within minutes they were both breathing quickly, grasping each other, arching, writhing, offering, pleading.

"Ah, sweetheart, I can't take any more of this," Kyle grated. "I planned to make this first time last all night, but that was one hell of a stupid idea. I can see that now. I need you too much. I've waited so long. I can't wait any longer." He leaned across her, fumbling with the drawer of the table that stood beside the bed. He grabbed a small foil packet and ripped it open.

"Please, Kyle. Please. Now. I want you. I've never felt this way before. *Please.*"

"Let me inside you," he muttered as he settled her onto her back and loomed over her. His eyes were glittering gemstones in the dark shadows. His face was a taut mask of desire. "I need to be inside you. I need to know you're mine."

She parted her legs for him again, her fingers digging into his shoulders as he moved quickly to take possession of her soft, womanly secrets. She held her breath as she felt him guide himself to the entrance of her body.

"Open your eyes, baby. Look at me. I want to see you looking at me when I take you." Kyle's fingers moved in her hair.

She lifted her lashes, knowing full well that she was revealing her need, her subtle, primitive, feminine fear of surrender and her love. When she met his gaze she struggled desperately to see beneath the surface of his hard, demanding desire. But it was impossible. His raging need dominated everything in that moment.

"I love you, Kyle," she said for the second time that night.

"Show me, baby. Take me inside and show me." He pushed into her abruptly, thrusting hard until he had lodged himself deeply within her. She welcomed him, crying out with soft pleasure. He drank the small sounds from her lips, savoring them.

He was still for a moment, his whole body taut with the effort. He waited until they had both adjusted to the intimate connection and then began to move.

Each stroke was slow, sure and as deep as Kyle could make it. Rebecca's head spun with sensation. Instinctively she lifted her hips to meet his thrusts. Kyle muttered against her throat, words of rough, driving sensuality. Rebecca shuddered in his tight hold, surrendering completely to the violent demands of the passion they had generated between them.

The culmination of their lovemaking seized them quickly, hurling them both into a whirlpool of convulsive release that seemed to go on forever. Kyle went rigid all over, and Rebecca dimly heard his half-strangled shout of triumph and satisfaction. She knew she was calling his name in a soft litany.

And then it was over, and Rebecca acknowledged to herself that the walls of her personal world, once so carefully structured, had been permanently breached. Nothing would ever be quite the same again for her.

An element of wildness had been introduced into her civilized world. And she knew that Kyle Stockbridge was the man she had been waiting for all her life.

It was a long time before Kyle could bring himself to roll clear of Rebecca's warm, soft body. Eventually, with a sigh of relaxed satisfaction he flopped onto his back and gathered her against his side.

He should probably tell her everything now, but he couldn't bring himself to do it. He told himself it didn't really seem like an appropriate time to start a long, involved explanation. Morning would be soon enough for the kind of story he had to tell. Right now he just wanted to enjoy the aftermath.

The future, now that he had time to think about it, appeared bright and beckoning. It was amazing how much more clearly he could think now that he had temporarily assuaged the compelling desire that had been growing in him for the past few weeks.

"Kyle?"

"Hmm?" He yawned magnificently.

"What are you thinking?"

"I'm thinking that you're the best thing that's happened to me in a very long time," he said honestly.

Rebecca smiled in the darkness and snuggled closer. "I'm glad. I was just thinking something similar about you."

He laughed indulgently, pleased by the small confession. "Good. Then you won't give me any static when I tell you what happens next."

She stilled. "What does happen next?"

He propped himself up on one elbow and looked down at her questioning face. She looked so gentle and sweetly sensual with her dark hair in a tangle around her shoulders. One shadowed nipple peeked up at him from the edge of the sheet. Kyle leaned over to kiss the inviting nubbin. He felt the faint ripple of response that went through Rebecca and luxuriated in it.

"I want you to move in with me," he told her quietly, raising his head to watch her reaction. "The sooner, the better."

Her eyes widened but she said nothing for a long moment. Kyle frowned when he realized she wasn't exactly leaping at the offer.

"Well?" he prompted forcefully.

"I don't know if that's such a good idea, Kyle," she finally said.

He was instantly outraged. It hadn't occurred to him that she might refuse him, not after the way she had just given herself so completely.

"What the hell does that mean?" he demanded, keeping a firm rein on his temper. He had promised himself he would never lose his temper with Rebecca. "On at least two occasions during the past hour you've told me you loved me. A few minutes ago you were calling my name as you went up in flames in my arms. I've known you for over two months. I know for a fact there's no one else in your life. I want you and you want me. So why don't you think it's a good idea for us to live together?"

She looked up at him uneasily, her small, white teeth closing briefly around her lower lip. "It's going to be difficult enough to keep our...our relationship quiet. If I actually move in with you, it's going to be impossible."

Outrage threatened to explode into something even more volatile. Kyle struggled to keep the emotion in check. He grasped her shoulders, pinning her gently but firmly to the bed. "Let's get something clear here. I have no intention of trying to keep our relationship a secret. Hell, I want the world to know about it. As of tonight, you're committed to me."

"Be reasonable," she said desperately. "Office romances are always awkward."

"Damn it, don't trivialize what we have by calling this an office romance. I want you to live with me. I want you to share my home and my life. And I want everyone, including the entire staff of Flaming Luck Enterprises, to know that."

"People will talk."

"Hell, they're already talking. I've told you that. Might as well give them something to talk about."

"Easy for you to say."

"If you're worried about being the subject of gossip, then relax," he retorted tightly. "I'll fire anyone who says a word out of line. Once a couple of loudmouths have been shown the door, you won't have a thing to worry about."

Her mouth trembled in a small smile. "You're so incredibly arrogant. Have you always gotten everything you've ever wanted?"

He stared at her, not sure how to answer that. "No," he said finally and offered no further explanation.

The brief flash of amusement faded from her

face. Her eyes were suddenly alive with shrewd curiosity. "What is it you once wanted and didn't get?" she asked softly.

Instantly he regretted the impulse that had driven him to an honest answer. "Never mind. It's not important. Stop trying to change the subject." He would have to watch himself around this woman. She was too perceptive. She was getting to know him too well. Already she could predict his moods and second-guess his demands on the job. If he wasn't careful, she would learn to read him even more intimately. Having her move in with him was risky, he realized suddenly.

But it was worth the risk, Kyle decided. He was prepared to throw caution to the winds if it meant having Rebecca firmly established in his life. He would count on the Stockbridge luck to keep him balanced on the high wire he was walking.

"Becky…"

"I'll think about it, Kyle," Rebecca said slowly.

"Not a chance," he vowed. "If I let you think about moving in with me, you'll talk yourself out of it. You can be as stubborn as I am. Say yes, Rebecca. Say it now. Tonight. Let me handle anything that develops at the office."

"Can you handle *anything* that develops there?" she asked dubiously.

"Of course I can," he exploded tightly. "I'm the boss!"

"Oh, that's right," she said with an air of mocking surprise, "I keep forgetting."

For an instant he thought she was serious. Then

he saw the mischief in her eyes and he groaned. "I can see why there might be some confusion on the topic," he said dryly. "A lot of people are beginning to wonder who's running things at Flaming Luck. The line of whining petitioners at your office door is several times longer than it is at mine these days."

"Only because you're such an ogre."

"Thanks. Well, at least you know you've got job security. I wouldn't dare get rid of you now. The rest of the staff would probably quit on me within five minutes."

"Tell me something, Kyle. If I refuse to move in with you, will I still have job security?"

He froze, anger flaring up once more. He controlled it. "That's a damned fool question."

"I have to know," she said simply.

"What kind of bastard do you think I am?" he demanded. "We both know you'd quit on the spot if I tried to use your job to coerce you into doing what I want."

"So if I refuse, you won't fire me?"

"Hell, no. I won't fire you. But I won't stop making love to you, either. And one of these nights you're going to stop worrying about what everyone at the office thinks, and you'll decide to trust me. You know it and I know it. It's inevitable. So why not say yes tonight?"

Her smile was soft and mysterious and edged with promise. "Yes," she said quietly.

Kyle held his breath, wondering if he'd heard right. He'd been preparing a few more arguments, readying whatever ammunition he could find to talk her into doing what he wanted. But the battle appeared to be over. He wouldn't need to fire another shot. Relief surged through him. She was his.

"Tomorrow is Saturday," he said. "We'll get you moved in this weekend." He wanted to consolidate his victory quickly before Rebecca started chipping away at it. He'd seen her in action before when he'd put his foot down at the office. She would give in very demurely, and then she'd find ways to tunnel underneath the edifice of his Big Decision until she had exactly what she wanted. On more than one occasion Kyle had found himself left with a presidential edict that had been subtly stripped of all its teeth.

She caught her breath. "This weekend? You're that sure?"

"I'm that sure," he said evenly.

"I don't do windows," she warned.

He laughed, settling back against the pillows. He pulled her over on top of him. "Don't worry. You've got plenty of other talents."

She crossed her arms on his chest. Her eyes were full of warmth and laughter. "Such as?"

He grasped her hips and maneuvered her downward so that she could feel the swelling shaft of his newly aroused manhood. "You've got a natural gift for taking care of a rather persistent problem I've had lately."

"I'm a great believer in utilizing one's natural talents."

She wriggled enticingly and Kyle drew a deep, steadying breath. "Love me, baby," he begged suddenly, his fingers twisting in her hair. "Make love to me until I can't think."

She stared down at him for an instant and something flickered in her gaze. It was as if she had reached some inner decision. And then to Kyle's joyous relief, she was suddenly all over him. Her lips were everywhere, tasting him, teasing him, driving him insane with need. Her hands followed, exploring his body with a sweet boldness that made him suck in his breath. She was soft and warm and exciting. Kyle gave himself up to the glorious thrill of being pleasured by Rebecca.

She lavished her love on him. Kyle had never experienced anything like it. He was soon drunk on the sensations she created within him and like any drunk, he couldn't think too clearly about the future.

Rebecca was his secret treasure, Kyle told himself, and he would guard her better than any mythical dragon had ever guarded its pile of gold.

His last thought later that night as he fell asleep with Rebecca beside him was that he would wait a little longer than he had planned to tell her everything. Tomorrow was too soon. She was too nervous now about how the news of their affair would be received at the office. She needed time to adjust to the relationship and to her new life with him.

And he thought he had a little more time to spare. After all, he was way ahead of the lawyers who were looking for Rebecca Wade. He'd gotten lucky, naturally. He'd turned her up almost immediately once he'd started hunting for her. The law firm was in no hurry. It would probably spend a few more weeks searching for her.

Yes, he had time. And he had the Stockbridge luck. He could afford to coast for a while and enjoy being loved by Rebecca Wade. By the time he got around to telling her the truth, she would be too deeply committed to him to care why he had come looking for her in the first place.

THREE

For the next ten days Kyle indulged himself completely in the myriad pleasures of living with Rebecca. He discovered he thrived on a real home life. It was the first time he had ever really experienced such a phenomenon and the quiet thrill of it all amazed him. He started leaving the office at five o'clock along with the rest of his staff for the first time since he had founded Flaming Luck Enterprises.

Kyle also discovered the rare pleasure of talking to a woman who understood him. Rebecca shared the day's events with him, bringing her insight and perspective to the after-work discussions that were held in his living room over a glass of wine.

Sometimes she chided him, and sometimes she applauded his business prowess. She frequently offered suggestions and was not backward about arguing a point.

Kyle liked the stimulation of talking business with Rebecca. He was not accustomed to confiding in a woman or anyone else for that matter, but he began to learn that doing so after a long day's work was a relief. Everything in his life seemed a little lighter around Rebecca.

Most amazing of all was that he was gaining a new perspective on the role of business itself in his world. He was learning that there were other priorities in life. Making love to Rebecca was at the top of the list.

On Thursday he was forced to leave town on a business trip that had been scheduled weeks in advance. The thought of being away from Rebecca for even one night disturbed him. He stopped by her office that afternoon on his way to catch the plane.

"Are you sure you don't want to come with me?" he demanded.

She smiled. "Kyle, we've already been through this. You need me here to coordinate the final stages of the Jennings-Hutton deal, remember? You said so yourself."

He swore softly and scowled. "I know. Damn it, I wish I could cancel this trip."

"You'll only be away one night," she pointed out gently.

He looked at her, unable to explain how crucial every single night was when a man was living on borrowed time. He had no way of knowing when the lawyers were going to catch up with her and he didn't want to waste a minute. "What are you going to do while I'm gone?" he asked.

"Go out partying with the boys from marketing, I think," she said musingly.

"You're going to do *what*?" He saw red for an instant. And then he saw the teasing laughter in her amber eyes. "Baby, don't ever make jokes like that, okay? It's dangerous."

"For who?"

"Guess," he retorted succinctly. "Now tell me the truth. What are you going to do tonight?"

"Go home, have a drink, have dinner and read that new thriller I bought the other day."

He nodded in satisfaction. "That's better. I'm going to miss you, Becky."

"I'll miss you, too." She got up from behind her desk and came around to slip into his arms. "Call me as soon as you get to the hotel in Phoenix, so I'll know you arrived safely."

Kyle grinned as he stroked her soft nape. The novelty of having to phone someone to let her know he was okay filled him with deep pleasure. He liked the sense of being tied to Rebecca. "I'll call right away."

"Promise?"

"Promise." Then he kissed her thoroughly and forced himself to leave before he missed the plane.

Hours later in Phoenix he reached for the bedside phone as soon as he got rid of the bellhop.

"I'm here," he announced. "Safe and sound. What are you doing?"

"Right this minute? I'm in the kitchen chopping some cabbage. What are you doing?"

"Getting hard."

Rebecca giggled on the other end of the line. "At the thought of me chopping cabbage? Now that's interesting. Is it the image of the knife in my hand, or the thought of my cute little apron that's turning you on?"

"The apron," he replied unhesitatingly. "I'm picturing you wearing it and nothing else."

"I'll wear it for you tomorrow night when you get back from Phoenix," she promised in a husky voice.

"Yeah." Kyle lounged against the pillows, aware of the tightness in his lower body. It was going to be a long night. "How'd everything go at work after I left this afternoon?"

"We all survived. Flaming Luck didn't go bankrupt or anything. Rick Harrison says he's got the Jamison deal under control."

"He'd better have it under control," Kyle retorted. "If he loses that one, I'll have his head and then I'll have your sweet little tush."

"My little tush?" she asked with innocent surprise.

"You bet. You're the one who talked me into delegating the responsibility for the Jamison deal to Harrison, remember? That project's important to me, Becky. If we don't get it, Clear Advantage Development will and I'm not about to let that happen."

"I see," she said lightly. "Well, goodness. If I'd known my tush was on the line, I might have thought twice about encouraging you to let Harrison have the responsibility for closing the deal."

Kyle grinned. "In the long run, it doesn't really matter."

"No?"

"Nope. I'm going to have your cute little tush, either way. Fill me in on the status of the Jennings-Hutton deal."

She did, eventually ending the conversation by telling him she would be at the airport to meet him. Kyle hung up the phone reluctantly and went to take a cold shower.

The next afternoon she was there in the waiting lounge just as she said she would be. Kyle couldn't remember the last time anyone had met him at the airport. When she came running forward to throw her arms around him, he was overcome by a wave of happiness.

They drove home where Rebecca had dinner and a bottle of wine waiting. Kyle felt as if he'd been dropped into a magic world where reality was temporarily suspended while he learned the heady little glories of domesticity.

Later that night Rebecca put on a frilly apron, just as she'd promised. She wore nothing underneath. Kyle thought he was going to go out of his mind.

When she shuddered delicately in his arms and cried out his name, he decided to wait just a little while longer before he told her the full truth. Normally a blunt, realistic man who met problems head-on, he discovered he couldn't bear to shatter the fragile illusion he'd created for himself.

The Stockbridge luck ran out the following Monday morning. When the dust had finally settled, Kyle reminded himself morosely that he should have known better than to trust the family luck when it came to women. It had traditionally worked well in matters involving cattle, mining and business but it had never been very reliable when it came to handling the female of the species.

The Stockbridge men had never been notably successful with women and Kyle's track record was the worst in three generations.

The fateful day had started out pleasantly enough. Kyle had awakened to find Rebecca's pretty little derriere nestled against his thighs. A jolt of early-morning arousal had whipped through him instantly.

No doubt about it—he had gotten spoiled in the past few days. With the familiarity generated by several other mornings of waking up in this position, Kyle had kissed Rebecca's shoulder and eased his hand down over her breast to the pleasant warmth between her legs. She had responded with sleepy sensuality, turning toward him instinctively without even opening her eyes.

It was the unhesitating way she turned to him whenever he touched her, regardless of the time of day or night, that Kyle had decided was one of the most pleasurable aspects of living with Rebecca Wade. In the past ten days he had hungrily explored the full range of her responses. It seemed to him that she was a creature of light and magic—a creature of soft, feminine heat and passion. Whenever he wanted her, she was there. When she made love to him, he felt as if he were the luckiest man in the world. She was his and Kyle had never had anything like Rebecca Wade before in his life.

She was unique. He was convinced she had been made especially for him, and he was determined to imprint himself on her so thoroughly that she would never look at another man. When he held her tightly in his arms and drank the soft cries of sexual release from her lips he was thrilled to the core of his being. He would do anything to keep her.

The new morning routine had established itself quickly. On the morning his luck finally failed, Kyle drove both Rebecca and himself to the office and parked the Porsche in the president's slot in the company lot. He left Rebecca at her office door, unperturbed that a junior clerk witnessed his goodbye kiss. Rebecca blushed and hurried into the office, scolding him gently for that sort of behavior on the job. She had to scold him every morning for the same reason.

But Kyle didn't care if the entire staff saw him kissing Rebecca. He walked on down the hall to his own office, whistling half under his breath as he rounded the corner and nodded to his secretary, Theresa Aldridge.

"Good morning, Theresa. How was your weekend?" He glanced at the mail she had been opening.

"Just fine, Mr. Stockbridge. And yours?" Theresa gave him a serenely polite smile that didn't quite succeed in hiding her laughing amusement. Theresa was fifty-three years old and she had been working for Kyle for nearly five years. Long enough to know that his behavior during the past ten days had revealed a whole new side to his character. She was very pleased, as if his relationship with Rebecca constituted some sort of personal victory for her.

"I had a great weekend, Theresa."

"I gather you didn't spend your weekend in the office, as usual Mr. Stockbridge. I didn't find any memos or instructions waiting for me this morning as I have on just about every other Monday morning for the past five years."

"You are correct, Theresa. I didn't spend my weekend in the office. I have discovered better things to do with my weekends."

"I'm happy to hear it."

"Did Harrison get the report on the Jamison deal finished?"

"Yes, sir. I have it here. He dropped it by a few minutes ago." She handed him the file.

"Thanks," he responded, flipping open the file as he walked toward the inner office. "Oh, by the way, Theresa, you don't have to bother bringing me a cup of coffee this morning. Becky fixed me a cup at breakfast," he added smugly.

"I see," Theresa replied aloofly.

Kyle grinned. Ever since Rebecca had declared that company secretaries should not be required to fix coffee for their bosses, Kyle and all his managers had found themselves engaged in a daily battle for the traditional perk. The secretaries were winning. They could afford to stand firm. They had Rebecca on their side.

Theresa had been as intransigent as all the other secretaries. It gave Kyle a certain satisfaction to be able to point out to her that the amazon who had led the resistance movement at the office had surrendered privately on the home front.

"Becky makes terrific coffee," Kyle added just to make sure he had made his point. He scanned the first page of the report, his mind switching gears as he started another working day.

"I'm sure she does," Theresa murmured behind him. "Miss Wade does everything well."

Something in her tone stopped Kyle for a moment. He swung around, eyes narrowing in a ferocious frown. "Just what is that supposed to mean, Theresa?" He was more than ready to jump down the throat of the first person who dared say anything critical about his relationship with Rebecca. So far he'd had no occasion to do so.

Theresa continued to smile at him, unalarmed by the frown. Theresa had, after all, worked very closely with Kyle for nearly five years. She knew him better than anyone else in the company. "Only that you seem quite happy these days, Mr. Stockbridge, and we all know it's because of Rebecca." She hesitated and then added in a soft rush, "I'm glad for you. It's about time you found other things to do with your weekends and evenings besides spend them here in the office building your empire."

Kyle nodded, satisfied that her congratulations were genuine. "Thank you, Theresa." He turned and continued on into his office. Rebecca had been wrong, he thought as he returned to Harrison's report. There had been no need for her to worry about what people at the office would say when it became common knowledge that she was living with him.

The truth was, nearly everyone who worked for him was damned grateful to her. She was in a better position than ever to soothe the savage beast.

Ten minutes later, however, Kyle's pleasant Monday-morning mood had vanished in the flames of outrage. He stared at the figures and conclusions buried in Harrison's report, certain at first that there had been a mistake or that he was reading them wrong. But a moment later he knew there had been no errors. He reached out and stabbed the intercom switch.

"Yes, Mr. Stockbridge?"

"Get Rick Harrison in here. Now."

"Yes, Mr. Stockbridge." Theresa's voice slipped into the smooth tone of the professional secretary who knows that disaster has just struck.

Kyle released the intercom switch and went back to the report. Then another thought struck him. He slammed the switch once more. "Theresa?"

"Yes, Mr. Stockbridge?" Theresa said warily.

"Tell Harrison that if he stops by Becky's office on the way to mine, I'll have his termination papers cut in personnel before lunch. Understood?"

There was a pregnant pause from Theresa's end before she said carefully, "I believe Mr. Harrison is already in Miss Wade's office, Mr. Stockbridge."

"The hell he is."

"Sir, it's normal Monday morning procedure," Theresa explained hurriedly. "Mr. Harrison always consults with her first thing on Monday. They go over your schedule for the week and prepare recommendations for you."

"Every Monday?" Kyle's outrage went up another notch. "Every damned Monday? How long has this been going on?"

"For about three weeks, sir," Theresa admitted and then tried frantically to do a little damage control. "Miss Wade has started a new program. She meets with the various department heads at different times during the week, Mr. Stockbridge. It's one of the ways she keeps things running smoothly for you. Monday morning just happens to be Mr. Harrison's scheduled time. I'll call her office right now and have her tell Mr. Harrison that you want to see him."

"You will not do any such thing, Theresa," Kyle told her with grim menace. "It'll be worth your job if you dial her office. I'll go down the hall and get Harrison myself."

"Yes, Mr. Stockbridge." Theresa's voice had moved from coolly professional to those special, frozen ranges only a good secretary can manage.

Kyle wasn't fooled for a minute. It would be a close race. He grabbed the report off his desk and headed for the door. Theresa was bent industriously over her electronic typewriter as he slammed through the outer office. He knew she would be reaching for the phone as soon as he cleared the doorway. He had about ten seconds.

He made it to the closed door of Rebecca's office just in time to hear the phone ring inside. Kyle shoved open the door without bothering to knock and surprised Rebecca just as she reached for her phone.

"Tell Theresa she's too late. I'm already here." He lounged in the doorway and shot Rick Harrison a disdainful glance. "Tell her nice try." Harrison sighed and leaned back in his chair with the air of a man who has just seen the jury return to the courtroom.

"How on earth do you know it's Theresa?" Rebecca asked mildly as she picked up the phone. As usual, she appeared totally unalarmed by Kyle's volatile mood.

"Lucky guess," Kyle said dryly. He slapped the file against his thigh and waited.

"Hello? Theresa? Oh, it is you. Mr. Stockbridge just walked in."

Rebecca's eyes stayed on Kyle's face as she

talked. He saw her wince as realization dawned. She was obviously putting two and two together in a hurry. Kyle grinned threateningly and glanced around the room.

Rebecca had done wonders with her small office, turning it from utilitarian to cozy. She had achieved the effect with a number of plants and a small Oriental carpet. There was a coffee machine in one corner. The leader of the coffee resistance movement set an example by brewing and serving her own.

Kyle glared at the two half-empty cups that sat on the desk. Rebecca had obviously made coffee not only for herself, but for Harrison.

This had been going on every Monday for three weeks? Kyle reflected. He'd been prepared to chew Harrison up one side and down the other for the mess he'd made of the Jamison deal. Now he felt more like tearing the man apart and tossing the pieces out onto the freeway.

Harrison started to reach for his coffee cup. A glance at Kyle's face made him stop. He looked more unhappy and resigned to his fate than ever. Kyle didn't move from the doorway as he waited for Rebecca to get off the phone.

"Thank you, Theresa," Rebecca said soothingly. "I'm sure Mr. Stockbridge will calm down once everything's been explained to him."

"Don't count on it," Kyle said bluntly as Rebecca replaced the receiver. He held up the file and looked at Rick Harrison. "What kind of garbage is this? How the hell did you screw up this badly? You and I went over every last penny of that offer. Jamison had agreed to everything. The deal was in the bag, Harrison."

"Jamison changed his mind," Rick said evenly as he got to his feet. "It's a little complicated, but I can explain."

"You damned well will explain," Kyle said through gritted teeth. "You should have been camped in my office waiting to do exactly that this morning. But that's not where I find you, is it, Harrison? Instead you're down here in Rebecca's office trying to put together a strategy for dealing with me. Haven't you got enough guts to face me on your own?"

Rick's face turned a dull red. His mouth tightened angrily. "I always meet with Becky at this time on Monday mornings. I was heading for your office next. I wanted to give you an opportunity to go over my report before we spoke."

"Bull. You were trying to hide behind a woman's skirts."

"Kyle," Rebecca cut in firmly, her voice soft but her eyes snapping with annoyance, "that's enough. You're jumping the gun here. Rick was on his way down to your office. He just stopped off here first because we have a scheduled Monday-morning meeting."

Kyle's eyebrows rose as he turned his attention back to her. He knew he was probably overreacting, but that was just too bad for everyone concerned. The flash of primitive male jealousy had taken him by surprise. The fact that there was probably no real basis for it didn't seem important at the moment. He felt an overpowering need to make his irritation clear.

"Don't leap to his defense, Becky, or I'll know for sure he was in here trying to get you to run interference for him. Harrison, go on down to my office and wait for me."

"Yes, sir." Rick got up and headed for the door.

"And the next time you decide to try hiding behind a woman's skirts," Kyle said very softly, "don't pick my woman."

Rebecca went still behind her desk. But Rick met Kyle's eyes in a man-to-man exchange. He nodded grimly as the full weight of his misfortune hit him. He disappeared out into the hall, closing the door behind him.

Somewhat mollified at having successfully intimidated his subordinate, Kyle turned back to Rebecca. He wasn't prepared for the anger glittering in her amber eyes.

"How dare you?" she whispered. "Kyle, that was utterly uncalled for. How could you drag that scene with Rick down to the personal level? How in the world am I supposed to work here if you act like this every time you find a man in my office? Of all the stupid, idiotic, dumb things to do... I *knew* this situation wasn't going to work." A pencil she had picked up snapped in two between her fingers. She tossed the pieces aside. "I just knew it wouldn't work. I should never have moved in with you. This whole thing is just impossible."

Kyle was startled by the force of her reaction. His own anger rekindled, but he kept a lid on it as he always did around Rebecca. He paced forward aggressively, tossed the Jamison file on her desk and planted both palms on the wood surface. "This wouldn't have gotten personal if I hadn't found Harrison sharing a cozy cup of coffee with you. What the hell is going on around here? Theresa tells me this is the order of the day on Monday mornings. Who are you seeing Tuesday mornings?"

"Sandra Billings from word processing," Rebecca shot back. "Are you going to label that unprofessional behavior, too? You think maybe Sandy and I sit in here and play cards or gossip about our love lives on Tuesday mornings?"

"Don't try to wriggle out of this by making it all sound perfectly normal."

"It is perfectly normal. This was the way I worked at Exton and Fordyce. The way my boss, Mr. Carstairs, liked me to work. It's effective and efficient. You liked the way I handled things there, remember? You said you were very impressed by what Carstairs told you about my performance. You said he raved about me. That's the reason you hired me when the firm got bought out, if you'll recall."

Kyle stomped down an irritating sense of guilt. Carstairs's recommendation, as enthusiastic as it was, had not been the deciding factor in Kyle's decision to hire Rebecca but he could hardly explain that now. He sought for another approach.

"I have no objection to your working methods," he bit out, "but I won't have the rest of the staff using you to hide from me. And that's exactly what Rick Harrison was trying to do this morning."

"That's not true!"

"It is true. Damn it, I know Rick and I know how everyone on my staff has started using you when they want to avoid having to face me."

"Rick and I were discussing your schedule this week, not the Jamison deal," Rebecca flared. "You're trying to make something very innocent appear underhanded and unprofessional."

"I don't like the idea of you having coffee every Monday morning with Rick Harrison."

"Your objections are ridiculous. You sound jealous, Kyle."

Her words cut deep. Kyle swore and swung away from the desk. He paced to the far end of the room and turned around to confront her. "Maybe I am," he admitted quietly.

Rebecca's expression softened instantly, just as he had known it would. Rebecca couldn't stand to see people in pain. She would be the last woman on earth who would try to make her lover jealous.

"You have no reason," she told him gently.

He looked at the second coffee cup on her desk. "Don't I?"

"Oh, Kyle, how can you say that?" Rebecca jumped to her feet and hurried around the edge of the desk, her eyes full of anguished concern. "You know I would never get involved with anyone else." She touched his arm as she looked up at him. "You do know that, don't you? I love you, Kyle. You do trust me, don't you?"

He gazed down into her anxious face for a long moment and magnanimously decided to let himself be placated. Kyle's mouth curved in a faint smile as he lifted his hand and stroked the curve of her throat with one knuckle. "I trust you, baby," he growled softly. He bent his head and brushed her mouth with his own. "But I'm not sure I trust Rick Harrison or the rest of the males around here. It makes me nervous to find out you're spending your mornings in here feeding them tea and sympathy."

"Coffee and a review of weekly plans are all that get served in here," she said firmly. "And I have to know you believe that, Kyle, or I won't be able to go on working here."

The small threat annoyed him. Kyle frowned, about to tell her he didn't want to hear anything more on the subject of her not being able to work for him, when the door opened with the barest of peremptory knocks.

"Excuse me, Miss Wade," Theresa Aldridge said brusquely as she sailed into the room. "I happened to be passing, and I thought I'd drop off your morning mail." She smiled challengingly at Kyle. "Hello, Mr. Stockbridge. I didn't realize you were still in here. Mr. Harrison is waiting for you in your office."

"Thank you, Theresa," Kyle said dryly as he stepped away from Rebecca. "I'm sure Miss

Wade appreciates your well-timed helpfulness."
He reached out and relieved his secretary of her
small burden. "Goodbye, Theresa. Tell Harrison
I'll be along in a minute."

"Of course. Anything else I can do for you,
Miss Wade?" she asked pointedly.

"I think that will be all, Theresa. Everything
seems to be under control now. Thanks for bringing the mail." Rebecca's golden eyes were warm
with rueful amusement as she moved back to her
desk.

"Any time," Theresa murmured as she backed
out of the door. She did not close it behind her.

Kyle watched his secretary depart and shook
his head in mocking disgust. "What the hell am I
going to do with my staff? Discipline is falling
apart around here. It was bad enough when they
got the idea they could use you to handle me.
Now they're starting to act protective around
you."

"I think it's rather sweet," Rebecca said as she
sat down. Her eyes were full of laughter.

"Sweet, my foot. How am I supposed to stay in
charge if my entire staff is on your side?" As he
walked toward the desk he automatically glanced
down at the small stack of letters he was holding.

The familiar name of the law firm in the upper
left-hand corner of the envelope on top leaped out
at him. Shock ricocheted through his whole body.
His stomach clenched. *Not now*, he thought. It
was too soon. He wasn't ready for this. He

needed a little more time. Just a few more days or weeks.

But his luck had run out.

"Is something wrong, Kyle?" Rebecca reached for her mail, glancing at the top envelope.

"No." The single word felt like a broken fragment of glass. Reluctantly he handed her the small stack of letters, watching with inner anguish as she fiddled with the top envelope.

There was nothing he could do about it now. He would talk to her tonight, Kyle told himself. He would wait until they got home. Then he would pour her a glass of wine and explain everything to her. She would understand. After all, she loved him. "I'd better get back to my office before Harrison starts to wonder if I'm going to let him off the hook."

"Listen to him before you start chewing on him, Kyle," Rebecca said seriously as she glanced up from the mail. "He's one of your best men. You owe him the courtesy of listening to his explanation."

Kyle looked at her. "That's good advice," he said finally. "Remember it when your turn comes." He walked out of the office without a backward glance.

Rebecca sat staring meditatively at her empty door. She was making progress, but the truth was there were still far too many occasions when Kyle turned into the unreadable, shadowed man she had first met two months and ten days ago. He was still very much a mystery to her in some ways even while in others he seemed to welcome the warmth and light of her love.

On the whole things had worked out better than she had thought they would. She had been uneasy with the situation right from the start, wary of getting involved not just because Kyle was her boss but because there were so many things she didn't know about him.

The thing she had fretted about most, namely the reaction of co-workers, had proven to be the least of her problems. As far as Rebecca could tell, everyone seemed to be watching the relationship with a fond eye, as if they had all been involved as matchmakers. There was talk, naturally, but it was amazingly devoid of maliciousness.

Kyle was no womanizer. He had, in fact, an amazingly pristine reputation for a man in his position and with his obvious heterosexual orientation. Rebecca had learned during the past several weeks that his employees respected that. It was probably the main reason they were so fascinated now with the relationship that had bloomed right under their noses.

Sometimes, though, in the middle of the night when she lay awake thinking about her uncertain future, Rebecca wondered if people would be so kind if the relationship exploded in her face.

The risk was definitely present. Rebecca was all-too aware of the fact that Kyle had never once told her he loved her. She'd convinced herself he would eventually be able to overcome whatever darkness prevented him from being able to give himself completely. She took heart from the fact that he had changed a lot in just the ten days she'd been living with him. It was true most of their intimate conversations still revolved around business, but she was working to change that.

She could only hope that he would someday realize the full depth of his feelings for her and admit them.

But there was always the possibility that she was deluding herself. She knew so little about him. She'd heard rumors of a broken engagement four years earlier, and someone had hesitantly mentioned that Kyle was said to have been married at one time. But Rebecca dismissed the last rumor as pure speculation.

That was the sum total of what Rebecca knew about Kyle's past.

Not much.

Rebecca sighed and picked up her mail. The envelope on top caught her eye. Few people welcomed letters from lawyers or the tax people. Warily she slit open the envelope wondering if she'd done anything recently that could get her sued. Doubtful. If Kyle's reputation was clean, hers could only be labeled pure to the point of dull. Getting involved with Kyle Stockbridge was the most adventurous thing she'd done in her entire life.

So why would a lawyer be trying to contact her?

She scanned the contents of the letter and learned two things immediately. The first was that she was not being sued. The second was that she was the sole heir of a distant relative she'd never even heard of until that moment—a certain Miss Alice Cork. The law firm handling Miss Cork's estate wished to discuss the terms of the will with Rebecca.

Rebecca sat dazed for a moment and then leaped to her feet and dashed out of her office.

"Hello, Theresa. Is Kyle in?" she asked as she breezed through the reception area of Kyle's office.

"He is, but he's still dining on Mr. Harrison. Care to wait?"

Rebecca grimaced. "I guess not. I have a weak stomach and there's no telling what that office will look like when Kyle's through with Rick. Would you leave a message for Kyle to call me when he's free?"

"Sure thing." Theresa eyed the letter in Rebecca's hand. "Good news?"

Rebecca laughed. "I don't know yet."

She went back down the hall, disappointed at not being able to share the excitement with Kyle. She phoned the law firm's office and made an appointment for later that afternoon.

"We're so glad to have finally located you, Miss Wade," the firm's secretary murmured. "Mr. Cramwell has been looking for you for nearly three months."

She learned very little over the phone, but she did manage to confirm that she was the right Rebecca Wade. There had been no mistake. Rebecca hung up the phone and determined to call her Aunt Beth later that evening. Aunt Beth was the family genealogist. She might know who Alice Cork was.

Kyle did not call all morning. By lunchtime Rebecca was practically bubbling with eagerness to tell him the amazing story. She picked up her purse and went down the hall to meet him. They had been having lunch together every day for the past ten days.

Kyle was just emerging from his office as Rebecca walked through the door. He was frowning, clearly preoccupied. He glanced at her as he shrugged into his jacket. "Oh, there you are, Becky. I was just going to have Theresa give you a call. We'll have to skip lunch today. I've got a meeting with Jamison at his club. I'm going to try to salvage the deal. See you later."

Rebecca blinked as he strode past her. Kyle paused long enough to drop a short, hard kiss on her mouth and then he was gone. "Good luck," she called after him, but she doubted if he'd heard.

She turned back to find Theresa studying her thoughtfully. Rebecca was disconcerted by the odd look in the secretary's eyes. "Well," she tried to say cheerfully, "did Rick survive?"

"Rick's alive and well as far as I know," Theresa said mildly. "But I can't quite figure out what's wrong with the boss."

"Something's wrong with Kyle?" Rebecca was startled.

"Beats me. All I know is that there's no meeting scheduled with Jamison. Not unless Mr. Stockbridge set it up by mental telepathy."

"Oh," said Rebecca. She retreated to the company cafeteria and wondered if the honeymoon was over already. Of course, she reminded herself bravely, one could hardly have a honeymoon if one wasn't married.

At two o'clock she took an hour off from work to meet with Alice Cork's lawyers. When she left their offices fifty minutes later, she was feeling stunned. She was now the proud owner of a fair-size wedge of land in the Colorado mountains.

At five o'clock Kyle finally showed up at her office door. He had his jacket slung over one shoulder and a bleak, challenging expression on his face, as if he were about to go into battle.

"Ready?" he asked.

Rebecca hesitated. "I'm not sure," she said honestly. "You look as though you're about to meet the sheriff at high noon out in front of the saloon. Is something wrong, Kyle?"

"Yeah, but we'll get it straightened out. Let's go." He turned away and started down the hall.

Rebecca seriously considered not following. The excitement of the news she had received earlier that afternoon was wearing off. Apparently she had bigger problems.

"Becky?" Kyle glanced back over his shoulder, scowling at her as he realized she wasn't trailing obediently after him.

She swallowed. "Coming, Kyle." She picked

up her purse and closed the office door behind her.

"I salvaged the Jamison deal this afternoon," were the only words he offered on the drive back to his high-rise condominium.

"Congratulations." Rebecca didn't try to break the silence that descended after that. Time enough to tell him her news later. He parked the Porsche in the garage. He still said nothing as they headed for the elevator.

"Sit down," Kyle instructed as he followed her into the condo. "I'll get us both a drink. We're going to need it."

"Why?"

"I have a story to tell you," he said. "And you're not going to like it. Just remember the advice you gave me earlier today about listening to explanations, okay?" He paused for a moment in the kitchen doorway. "And remember something else, too, Becky."

"What?" she asked, aware of a cold chill somewhere in the vicinity of her stomach.

"Remember that whatever else happens, you and I are involved and that's not going to change. We'll get through this together."

FOUR

"I know all about the news you got from the lawyers this afternoon." Kyle stood at the window, drink in hand, staring broodingly out toward the mountains. "Congratulations."

"You don't sound all that thrilled for me," Rebecca remarked quietly. She clutched her glass of wine and waited for the ax to fall. She could almost hear it swishing through the air above her head.

"I'm not. It complicates matters. On the other hand, if it hadn't been for that land you inherited from Alice Cork, I would never have met you."

Rebecca took a deep breath. "How do you know about Alice Cork and the land?"

"It's a long story."

"Once upon a time…?" she prompted dryly.

"Right. Once upon a time." He paused, apparently searching for words. "Once upon a time there were two men and two ranches divided by one very valuable strip of land. The land in the middle was called Harmony Valley. It was badly named, to say the least. There has never been any harmony connected with that damned valley."

"Who owned Harmony Valley?"

"Each of the owners of the two ranches wanted it right from the start, but a man named MacIntosh actually got it first."

"And who owns the ranches that border it?" Rebecca asked with a strong sense of foreboding.

"The Ballards own Clear Advantage ranch, which borders one side of the valley."

"Clear Advantage?" Rebecca stared at Kyle's back. "Any connection with Clear Advantage Development Company?" The firm was one of Flaming Luck's arch competitors.

"There's a connection, all right. The same kind of connection that exists between Flaming Luck Enterprises and Flaming Luck ranch. I own both. Glen Ballard owns the Clear Advantage and the development company he's built. He named his company after the family land, just as I did. Our ranches both border Harmony Valley. The Ballards and the Stockbridges have been feuding over that damned valley for three generations."

Rebecca got a queasy sensation in her stomach. "Feuding?"

Kyle turned to face her. His green-and-gold eyes were riveting in their intensity. "It started with a woman and a piece of land, and it looks like it's going to end that way."

Rebecca set down her glass with a very deliberate movement and clasped her hands in her lap. "You'd better tell me about it."

Kyle hesitated and then began to recite the tale with the fluency of someone who has heard the story many times since childhood. "The Ballards and the Stockbridges both wanted Harmony Valley. Originally because of the water. Later because of the mining potential. MacIntosh, the original owner of Harmony Valley, wouldn't sell to either the Ballards or the Stockbridges. From all accounts he was a tough old bastard. Things got nasty. Threats were made. Shots were fired."

"That sounds like something right out of the Old West."

Kyle gave her an odd look. "It was the Old West. At any rate, MacIntosh finally offered a solution. He was dying and he had a daughter. She wasn't very pretty, I'm told, and she had no suitors. MacIntosh wanted her safely married off to either a Stockbridge or a Ballard. Whichever family accepted her as a bride got the land."

"That poor woman," Rebecca exclaimed in sympathy.

"She would have been rich, regardless of which side she chose."

"She would have been used."

"I hate to break this to you, Becky," Kyle said harshly, "but the fact is, people have frequently married for land."

"Go on with your story."

"Well, needless to say, the MacIntosh woman was courted by both sides. She eventually chose a Stockbridge. The Ballards were furious and things got increasingly violent as the wedding approached. Cattle got rustled, men got into fights in town and waylaid in the mountains. Inevitably a few folks got killed. Both sides were arming themselves for all-out warfare when the MacIntosh woman finally realized just why she was being married."

"You mean she didn't know? She honestly thought this ancestor of yours loved her?"

Kyle shrugged. "She was a young thing. Her father hadn't bothered to tell her the truth, figuring she'd be happier not knowing just why she was suddenly being courted by the two most eligible men for miles around. But it didn't take long for her to figure things out. And when she did, she was furious."

"She was hurt," Rebecca interjected fiercely.

"Whatever. At any rate, she kept her mouth shut and insisted on delaying the wedding as long as possible. Her father finally died. The day after the funeral, she called off the wedding. She now owned Harmony Valley free and clear, and she announced she wasn't going to marry anyone with the last name of Ballard or Stockbridge."

Rebecca looked up, absurdly pleased by the unknown woman's fortitude. "Good for her."

Kyle glared at her. "She started a feud that's still going on."

"She didn't start it. She was a victim of it. What happened next?"

"The MacIntosh woman finally married. She chose an outsider, someone from Denver. His name was Cork."

"Someone who loved her, I hope."

"Probably someone who wanted Harmony Valley," Kyle said grimly. "Good grazing land and a year-round water supply. However, he cared enough about the MacIntosh woman and her land to respect her wishes. He refused to sell, no matter how much the Ballards and the Stockbridges offered."

"Or threatened?"

"Probably. But Cork and his wife held out against both families. They eventually had children. Two died in infancy. The third, a daughter, lived to inherit the land."

"And promptly found herself overwhelmed by threats and offers of marriage from the next generation of Ballards and Stockbridges, I presume?"

Kyle nodded, his eyes shadowed. "All of which she refused at first. Her mother had taught her well, it seems. But she eventually got herself seduced by a Ballard. The Ballard charm is legendary in that part of the mountains. According to the story, she thought she was in love and that this particular Ballard was different. When she found out she was pregnant, she accepted his offer of marriage."

"What happened?" Rebecca realized she was becoming strangely fascinated by the bizarre tale.

"Shortly before the wedding she discovered the Ballard she was about to marry had a mistress, one he did not intend to give up after the wedding."

"So he was just marrying the Cork woman for Harmony Valley," Rebecca concluded sadly.

"You don't have to get emotionally involved in all this," Kyle said sharply. "It's ancient history."

"History, they say, has a way of repeating itself. What happened to the Cork woman?"

"She followed in her mother's footsteps. She called off the wedding at the last minute."

"Even though she was pregnant? In that day and age, that took guts," Rebecca said with admiration.

"Ballard was furious from all reports. Claimed he was the father of her child and she had to marry him. But she refused to admit the baby was his. Said it could just as easily be a Stockbridge bastard which, according to my father, was an outright lie. As it turned out, her pregnancy was a moot point. She miscarried shortly afterward and spent the next forty years of her life alone in Harmony Valley. Her name was Alice."

"My Alice Cork?" Rebecca asked swiftly. "The one I'm supposedly related to?"

"One and the same. She was one stubborn old lady. I'll tell you that much. Wouldn't give an inch. When Dad died and I took over the ranch, I went to see her about Harmony Valley. She wouldn't let me in the front door. The only satisfaction I had was that she was even less hospitable to Ballards. Three months ago she died."

"And left the land to me?" Rebecca shook her head in bewilderment. "But I never knew her. According to the lawyer, the relationship is very distant.''

''Which explains why it took so long for the lawyers to find you.'' Kyle took a swallow of his drink. ''Then again, lawyers are inclined to move slowly. I knew they wouldn't give the hunt for you top priority. After all, the client was dead and the firm was busy with more pressing matters. I, on the other hand, hired the best private investigation firm money can buy as soon as I saw the terms of the will.''

''How did you happen to see the will?''

Kyle sighed. ''Alice Cork instructed her lawyer to publish the whole damned thing in the newspaper that serves the community she'd lived in all her life. Her idea of a joke, no doubt. She wanted to be sure everyone in town knew the Stockbridges and the Ballards had been beaten once again by a woman. Anyway, I told the investigation firm there would be a bonus in it if they turned you up before the lawyers did.''

Rebecca's hands tightened into a fierce knot. ''You always move fast when you've got your goal in sight. I've worked with you long enough to know that.''

Kyle's mouth thinned. ''The end of the story is that I found you first. I got lucky. Stockbridges are known for their luck in, uh, certain areas. It turned out you were right here in Denver, working for a firm that I knew was about to be bought out. It was a simple matter to get an introduction through Carstairs. I've known him for years. And when I told him I could use an administrative assistant like you, he fell all over himself recommending you. He was concerned about your future after the buy-out."

Rebecca inhaled slowly. "And I, knowing my job was in serious jeopardy because of the buy-out, couldn't get over how lucky I was to run into you when I did. I was so grateful to you that I decided I'd make the best executive assistant you'd ever had."

"I've never had an executive assistant before," Kyle pointed out wryly.

"True. So I fulfilled my end of the bargain, didn't I? I was the best assistant you've ever had. Tell me, Kyle, when did you decide to seduce me?"

His eyes narrowed dangerously. "I didn't set out to seduce you, Becky. In fact, I wasn't sure what to do with you at first. The chief priority had been to find you, but once I'd accomplished that I wasn't sure how to handle you. You weren't quite what I was expecting."

"What were you expecting?"

"I don't know." Kyle moved restlessly. "You just took me by surprise, that's all. I'd hoped to find someone I could do business with, but the minute I met you I no longer wanted to do business with you."

"You expect me to believe that now? After hearing your family's history?"

He gave her a fierce, slanting glance. "Damn it, Becky, I didn't expect the attraction between us. I wasn't prepared for it. I decided to stall. I kept telling myself the lawyers would take months to find you, and in the meantime I could get to know you. I took things one step at a time. You needed a job. I was in a position to give you one."

"Figuring I'd be so grateful later I'd let you have the land at whatever price you chose to offer?"

Kyle looked down at the contents of his glass. When he looked up again, his eyes were blazingly honest. "It occurred to me that you might return the favor I'd done for you by listening to my offer for the land before you listened to Ballard's."

"Then I can definitely expect an offer from Ballard?" she asked coolly.

"You can bet Glen Ballard will be right on the lawyer's heels. He's always hanging around in the wings, waiting to steal the prize someone else has found."

Rebecca was shaken by the bitterness in the words. Her eyes widened. "I take it you've been through this sort of situation before with Ballard?"

"One or twice."

"When? Over business issues?" She was consumed with curiosity now. She'd never seen that look in Kyle's eyes before. It frightened her.

"Never mind, Becky. It's not important now. Right now all I want to do is get everything on the table between us. I realize this whole situation must seem a little confusing to you. I'm sure you've got some questions."

Rebecca shook her head slowly in amazement. "Trust you to try to make it all sound like a minor business arrangement that needs to be clarified. I've only got one real question for you, Kyle."

"Ask," he invited magnanimously. There was a certain amount of speculation in his gaze, as if he were fairly certain he had things under control now.

"What made you think you could get away with doing this to me?"

He stared at her. "What are you talking about? I haven't done anything to you except make love to you."

"You haven't made love to me," she said with soft scorn. "You've used me. You're no better than your ancestors. You tried to seduce me in the hopes of getting me to turn over the land without a fuss."

Kyle took a step forward. "Becky, that's not true. When you've had a chance to settle down, you'll realize that. I'm warning you. Don't make a lot of accusations now that you'll have to eat later. I've told you the truth about the way it happened. Our relationship now has nothing to do with Harmony Valley."

She got to her feet, so consumed with fury that she was surprised she wasn't going up in flames. "Don't stand there and lie to me, Kyle. It has everything to do with that valley. In fact, that valley appears to be the sole basis of our relationship. It's the reason we met in the first place, the reason you made love to me, the reason you asked me to move in with you. I'll give your ancestors credit for one thing—they at least offered marriage to the woman who owned the valley. I didn't even get that much!"

Kyle's green eyes glinted. "Rebecca, sit down. You're overreacting. This isn't like you. Calm down and give us both a chance to talk this out."

"What's to talk about? Do you want to buy that land from me?"

"Forget the land," Kyle snarled, his temper obviously beginning to fray. "We're not talking about the land, we're talking about us. You and me."

"Is that right? Then you'd have absolutely no objection if I gave the land away to Glen Ballard this afternoon?" she taunted.

Kyle brushed the threat aside with an impatient movement of his hand. "Don't make rash, stupid statements like that. You're just a little upset."

"*A little upset?*" She couldn't believe what she was hearing.

"Becky, we can deal with Harmony Valley later. It's not important right now. Our relationship is the important thing."

"What relationship?" She glanced wildly around. "As far as I can see, the only relationship we have exists because of that land."

"That's not true, damn it. Becky, listen to me." Kyle took two long strides forward and put his glass down. "You're being irrational. It's not like you. Just calm down and give yourself a chance to think."

Her chin came up. "What should I think about, Kyle? The fact that you've never once said you love me? The fact that I've been a fool thinking that you were falling in love with me and just needed time to understand your own feelings? Or maybe I should sit around and think about how I've been set up and used. Something tells me that would be a lot more productive."

"You were not being set up." His hands closed around her shoulders. He gave her a small shake. His gaze was brilliant as he controlled his anger with obvious effort. "You're not going to get away with accusing me of that, no matter how furious you are. I've told you once and I'll tell you again, our relationship has nothing to do with that land."

"I'm supposed to believe that?" She was incredulous. "After the story you've just told me?"

"Believe it, Rebecca," Kyle said through his teeth.

"Give me one good reason."

"You want reasons?" he shot back, "I'll give you a few—you owe me a little trust, Rebecca Wade. I'm the man you're sleeping with. The man you say you love."

"Why should I throw good love and trust after bad? At least I know now why you've never told me that you loved me. I'll give you some credit for honesty in that department."

His hands tightened roughly on her shoulders.

"I've given you everything I have to give a woman," he rasped. "Everything."

"Well, I've got news for you, Kyle Stockbridge. It's not enough." Rebecca stepped away from him quickly, taking several steps back as his hands fell to his sides.

"Don't run from me, Becky," he ordered softly.

"I do not run from anything or anyone. But I am going to get as far away from you as possible."

"I'll come after you."

She read the implacable intent in his eyes and smiled grimly. "You won't follow me for long. As soon as I get rid of Harmony Valley, you'll forget all about me. Don't worry about it, Kyle. Whatever you think you feel for me will vanish into thin air as soon as the land is no longer between us." She whirled and started down the hall to the bedroom.

Kyle was after her in a flash, hard on her heels as she hurried down the hall. "Where do you think you're going?"

"To a hotel tonight. Tomorrow I think I'll take a little trip up into the mountains. I'm curious to see the land that Alice Cork and her mother fought so hard to hang on to."

"They didn't want to hold on to Harmony Valley so much as they wanted to keep it out of Stockbridge or Ballard hands," Kyle said.

"Well, I can certainly understand them not wanting a Stockbridge to get hold of it. But, I, for one, have nothing against Ballards yet. Perhaps this Glen Ballard doesn't take after his ancestors the way you take after yours."

"Stop issuing vague threats, Becky. It's not your style."

"Who's threatening?" She rounded the corner into the bedroom and went to the walk-in closet to drag out her suitcase. When she swung around, she collided with Kyle who was almost on top of her. The edge of the suitcase caught him squarely in the midsection.

Kyle sucked in his breath, wincing. "Believe me, Rebecca, Glen Ballard is just as big a bastard as his father and his grandfather. I know it for a fact."

"Is that right?" Rebecca dumped the suitcase onto the bed, opened it and began tossing clothes into it willy-nilly. "How do you know that? What's he ever done to you except fight for the same business deals you wanted?"

"He seduced the woman I was engaged to marry, for one thing," Kyle said in a voice so cold it could have frozen hellfire.

Rebecca was so shocked she didn't move for an instant. She stared at Kyle, her arms full of lingerie. "Ballard stole your fiancée?" she finally repeated blankly.

"He and Darla have been married for nearly four years."

Rebecca moved slowly back to the open suitcase and dropped the lingerie inside. "I'd heard rumors that you'd been engaged once. No one said much about it."

"No one at work knows much about it," Kyle retorted. "It's not something I talk about on the job."

"Or anywhere else. I wondered when you'd get around to mentioning it." She closed the suitcase, locking it with unnecessary precision. "I heard rumors of a marriage, also. I dismissed the stories as idle gossip at the time. Now I'm not so sure. Is the tale true, by any chance, Kyle? Have you been divorced?"

He raked his fingers through his hair. "Yeah."

"Yeah? That's all the explanation I get for one divorce and a broken engagement?"

His eyes burned into hers. "What do you want me to say? That I'm a two-time loser when it comes to women? All right. I'll admit it. Stockbridge men don't make good husbands. Just ask anyone who knows us. The Stockbridge luck doesn't seem to apply when it comes to women," he concluded bitterly.

"Maybe the Stockbridge men shouldn't have relied on their luck when it comes to women. Maybe they should have tried being honest, instead." Rebecca picked up the suitcase. It was so heavy she had to use two hands to carry it.

"Put that down, Becky. You're not going anywhere."

"How are you going to stop me? Brute force? Don't try it, Kyle. It didn't work with the other women who owned Harmony Valley and it's not going to work with me. Get out of my way."

He closed his eyes briefly, obviously struggling

for self-control. "I don't want to let you leave, Becky. I'm afraid you'll do something crazy."

"Like what? Sell the land to Glen Ballard? I promise to let you know the minute I do. *Now get out of my way.*"

"You said you loved me, Becky," he reminded her very softly.

"Talk about doing something crazy," she muttered. "Stand aside, Kyle."

"This morning you lectured me on giving Harrison a chance to explain himself. I followed your advice. I listened to him."

"Don't draw any parallels. You've already had your chance to explain yourself and I didn't like the explanation."

"Damn it, Becky, you owe me a little trust."

"Why? Because I've been sleeping with you for ten days?" she shot back, enraged. "I don't owe you a thing for that privilege. As far as I'm concerned, you're the one who owes me. You owe me for all the love I've wasted on you. For all the love I was going to squander on you in the future. But it doesn't look like I'm ever going to get paid back, so I'll just have to write the whole mess off as a bad debt."

"Becky, I'm warning you. If you leave now, you'll regret it."

Her brows rose. "Is that right? What will you do? Fire me? Go right ahead. If Carstairs recommended me so enthusiastically to you, I'm sure I can get him to recommend me to someone else. Maybe Glen Ballard could use a good executive assistant who's been inside the enemy camp for over two months."

She'd gone too far with that last, empty threat. Rebecca understood that at once. Kyle's hand closed around her arm, his fingers locked in a punishing grip. But that grip wasn't nearly as unnerving as the bleak anger in his eyes.

"Don't even think about going to Glen Ballard," Kyle said far too softly.

Rebecca drew a steadying breath and decided that, as angry as she was, she couldn't bring herself to let this particular threat stand. She simply couldn't hurt the man she loved that much. "Relax, Kyle. I won't offer my services to your competitor. I have no interest in staying in the middle of this feud. I just want out. From the sounds of it, the quicker I get rid of that land, the better."

Kyle searched her face before reluctantly releasing her arm. "Sell the land to me and it will no longer be an issue between us, Becky," he urged with rough gentleness. "When the deal is concluded, you'll see that our relationship is independent of it. I'll still want you as badly as I do now. Nothing will change between us."

She couldn't help but marvel at the sheer scope of his nerve. "You don't ask much, do you?"

"Just your trust."

"And what do I get out of it?"

He frowned. "Everything you've had until now. Our relationship will return to the way it was until this morning."

"I hate to tell you this, Kyle, but I'm afraid

things can never go back to the way they were between us. Too much has happened. I want more than you can give. I know that now."

"Damn it, lady. What do you want from me?" His voice was raw.

"Love, commitment, open communication, the works."

"I've told you, Becky, I've already given you more than I've ever given any other woman."

"More than you gave your ex-wife or this Darla person you were engaged to once?"

"Leave my ex-wife and my ex-fiancée out of this."

"Why should I? You claim you've given me more that you've given any other woman, but you gave them rings. That's more than I've got. Goodbye, Kyle."

She glanced only once at his stricken expression as she pushed past him. It was too painful to dwell for long on his ravaged face. She was already hurting so much that she wanted to cry.

With a fierce effort of will Rebecca managed to lug the heavy suitcase down the hall, into the elevator and into the garage where her car was parked.

She was aware of Kyle following her silently every step of the way. He didn't offer to help with the heavy suitcase, but he made no effort to stop her as she got behind the wheel of the compact, either. He just stood in the entrance of the elevator lobby, his hands jammed into his pockets and watched as she turned the key in the ignition.

Rebecca's last glimpse of him in her rearview mirror revealed the implacable, unreadable face of a man who was accustomed to being alone—a man who hadn't really, deep down, expected to escape a lonely future.

There had been moments during their short time as a couple when Kyle had not looked so aloof and alone.

There had been times when Kyle had looked like a man who was falling in love. Rebecca told herself she must have been mistaken.

Three blocks from the condominium, Rebecca pulled into the parking lot of a grocery store and let the tears fall.

FIVE

It was the kind of summer day that had made the Colorado Mountains famous. The air was crystal clear, the sun dazzling on distant snow-capped peaks. The trees grew right down to the edge of the serpentine highway.

Rebecca took little pleasure in the magnificent scenery. She was intent on reaching her destination, a small town buried in the mountains. From there, the lawyer had told her, it was only a short drive to Harmony Valley. The keys to the house Alice Cork had lived in alone for so many years were in the bottom of Rebecca's purse.

Rebecca had not bothered phoning Theresa to inform her she would not be in to work today. She figured Kyle could handle that problem. It would be interesting to see how he explained his lack of knowledge of her whereabouts. The whole staff, after all, was well aware of the recent change in the boss's living arrangements.

Knowing Kyle, though, he probably wouldn't bother to make an excuse for his missing executive-assistant-live-in-lover. And no one would dare question him directly. Speculation would run rampant. And the staff was loyal enough to Rebecca now for the gossip to easily turn against Kyle.

That thought brought Rebecca little satisfaction. She was still dealing with the open wound Kyle had inflicted on her. She had no sympathy to spare for the man who had caused it. Kyle probably wouldn't give a damn if his whole crew began fulminating against him, anyway. Little things like that didn't bother Stockbridge.

But she had been unable to get Kyle's bleak, closed expression out of her mind. No matter how hard she tried, she'd been haunted by the shuttered, isolated look she had last seen on his face.

It had seemed for a while that Kyle was emerging from the shadows that surrounded him. But the events yesterday had proved he was as shrouded in them as ever.

A two-time loser, he had called himself. Rebecca shook her head in dismay. No wonder the man hadn't bothered to mention marriage. He was probably willing to marry to get the land, just as his father and grandfather had been, but with his record Kyle must have figured he had a better chance at a simple seduction than at a proposal.

Besides, Rebecca reminded herself bitterly, a live-in relationship was a lot easier to end than a more formal arrangement. Kyle was probably tired of terminating marriages and engagements.

He'd had too much experience in that department already.

Rebecca chided herself for the anguished uncertainty she had been enduring since the scene in Kyle's condo. He had wanted her trust but he had no right to demand it, she told herself. What had he given her in exchange for the love and trust she'd already given him?

He'd kept his secrets well. She wondered how much longer he would have remained silent about Harmony Valley and Rebecca's role in a feud that spanned three generations. Kyle must have known time was running out on him. Yet he had stalled right up until the lawyer's letter had landed on Rebecca's desk.

That wasn't like Kyle, she reflected. He was a man of action.

It was almost as if he hadn't wanted to deal with the situation he himself had created. It was as if he'd been crossing his fingers and hoping his luck would hold out. He had trusted to fortune that everything would go smoothly instead of blowing up in his face.

The Stockbridges were known for their luck, he'd said.

In certain matters.

Rebecca could well believe in the Stockbridge luck when it came to business, although she would have said it was luck based on a certain aggressive boldness, a savvy intelligence and shrewd instincts. A gunfighter's luck.

She'd been right when she'd first decided that

Kyle Stockbridge had been born in the wrong era. He belonged back in a more lawless time when men made their own rules out here in the Colorado wilderness.

Rebecca made good time. The small town named on the lawyer's page of directions hardly warranted the label. It consisted of little more than a couple of gas stations, a café, a grocery store, tavern and one tiny motel.

Rebecca decided she had little choice in the matter. She checked into the motel and considered herself fortunate. If the place had been full she would have had to drive on to the next town which was some distance away.

The room was paneled in fake wood, making the small space seem even darker and more confining that it already was. But the facilities worked and the bed was not as lumpy as it might have been under the circumstances. Rebecca unpacked her clothes and went in search of a bite to eat.

She had all afternoon to find Harmony Valley, she told herself. Now that she was near her goal, she wasn't quite so intent on reaching it. A part of her was suddenly reluctant to come face-to-face with the land that had destroyed her relationship with Kyle Stockbridge.

The café was filled with men wearing battered cowboy hats and caps that bore the famous logos of the makers of farm machinery. Rebecca was treated to a series of curious stares as she made her way to the one empty booth at the back. She suppressed a small smile. Strangers were obviously a rarity around these parts.

She took a seat and picked up the menu. It struck her that this miniscule burg was Kyle Stockbridge's hometown. Somehow it didn't seem odd that Kyle came from a place like this. She could envision him growing up in these mountains, becoming as hard and forbidding as the Rockies themselves.

"Hamburger and fries, please," Rebecca said to the waitress who came to take her order.

"Cheese?" the young woman asked, tossing her ponytail back over her shoulder. The gum she was chewing snapped cheerfully.

"Yes, please. And a cup of coffee."

"Be right back."

The waitress turned her head as a murmur of recognition and welcome went through the café.

Rebecca glanced toward the door along with everyone else and stiffened with shock.

"Hey," the waitress said with a pleased grin. "That's Kyle Stockbridge. Haven't seen him around here for ages." She waved enthusiastically, and her gum snapped again. "How you doin', Kyle?"

It was Kyle, all right, but not the Kyle Rebecca was familiar with. He wasn't dressed in a business suit, for one thing. He was wearing a pair of faded, snug-fitting jeans, a denim shirt and old, scarred boots. He had a black Stetson pulled down low over his eyes. It was obvious he was on familiar turf. He walked with the long, easy stride of a man who has spent time in the saddle and in the mountains.

There were a variety of friendly nods and laconic greetings as Kyle made his way down the aisle to Rebecca's booth. Strangers might be treated to cool, assessing stares around here, she thought wryly, but someone with roots in the area obviously got a different sort of welcome.

A part of her was thrilled to see him. The wave of longing that went through Rebecca made her dizzy for a moment before she managed to clamp a lid on her errant emotions.

But she knew from the gleam of satisfaction in Kyle's eyes that she had betrayed herself for a dangerous instant.

"Hello, baby," he said smoothly as he took the seat across from her. "Surprised to see me?"

"Yes," she said tightly.

"You shouldn't be. You must have known I'd follow you to Timbuktu."

"This isn't Timbuktu."

He smiled faintly as he set his hat down beside him on the red plastic upholstery. "True. But it is the only café in town. I checked at the motel and they said you were having lunch. It wasn't hard to find you. Don't forget, I've found you before under more difficult circumstances."

"You followed me," she accused softly.

"That's why you make such a good executive assistant, Becky. You're so sharp. So alert to the little nuances of a situation. So intuitive. Yes, ma'am, you're right. I followed you. What are you having for lunch?"

"A hamburger."

"Wise choice. I appreciate your not embarrassing me by trying to order pasta or Cajun chicken here. I'd be laughed out of town." He glanced up at the young waitress who had appeared at his side with a pot of coffee. "I'll have a burger, too, Jan. Make it rare."

"Sure, Kyle." She poured his coffee first and then poured Rebecca's. "You stayin' around long this trip?"

"Depends."

Jan slanted him a knowing look. "We all expected you to show up right after Alice Cork died. Dad said he expected you and Glen Ballard to ride into town with guns blazing. Thought the two of you would shoot it out in front of Pat's gas station. Just like in the movies."

"Not much point." Kyle looked at Rebecca. "Had to find out who had inherited Harmony Valley first."

Jan's eyes went to Rebecca's face in open speculation. "Are you the one?" she asked with eager curiosity. "We've all been wondering who Alice would stick with the problem of that valley. Who are you?"

"Meet the new owner of Harmony Valley," Kyle said blandly. "Her name is Rebecca Wade. She's my administrative assistant at Flaming Luck Enterprises. And," he added with calm possessiveness, "she's the lady I live with."

Rebecca's fingers trembled with the force of her anger. "Not any longer," she bit out.

But the damage was done. Ears perked up in nearby booths. Jan was staring at her, curiosity turning to outright wonder.

"Well, I'll be." Jan grinned at Kyle. "I guess this answers the question of who's finally gonna get Harmony Valley, huh?"

"Don't bet the café on it," Rebecca murmured. "I'd appreciate it if you'd put my order in, Jan. I'm getting hungry."

"Yes, ma'am." Jan was brimming with excitement as she hurried off to the kitchen. It was only too obvious she couldn't wait to be the bearer of fresh gossip.

"And I thought the talk would be bad at work." Rebecca glared at Kyle as she picked up her coffee cup.

"Folks around here have gossiped about Stockbridges and Ballards for three generations," Kyle observed. "Don't worry about it. Stockbridges and Ballards sure don't."

"Easy for you to say. You're the one who started the talk about me."

"People were bound to talk about you. This way they'll at least get the facts straight."

"Not from you, they won't. You just told Jan an outright lie. As of yesterday I am not living with you."

"Do you want to drive out to Harmony Valley right after we eat?" Kyle asked conversationally.

Rebecca fought her temper. She'd seen Kyle use

this tactic before. When he didn't care for the direction a conversation was taking, he simply changed it. It would be useless to try to force him to acknowledge the error of his ways.

"There is no 'we' about it. I intend to drive out to the valley after lunch. Alone."

"I'll take you. You're liable to get lost if you go by yourself."

"Then I'll get lost. It will be my tough luck."

Kyle gave her a level look. "I'll take you out to Alice's place, Becky."

She knew it was a losing battle, but something made her struggle on to the last ditch. "And if I decline your offer?" she inquired dryly. Kyle was always willing to let you know how big the club that he was holding over your head was.

"I'll follow you," he said simply.

The thought of wandering around unknown roads for miles searching for the lawyer's vague reference points while the black Porsche hovered in her rearview mirror was daunting.

"So kind of you to go out of your way like this," Rebecca said scathingly.

"My pleasure." Kyle paused, looking thoughtful. "Have I ever really been unkind to you, Becky? Be honest, honey."

"Here come our hamburgers," Rebecca announced. She was not above changing the direction of the conversation herself.

Kyle told himself the Stockbridge luck might be kicking in again. About time. Rebecca was obviously not pleased about the situation, but at least she was sitting beside him in the Porsche and she wasn't yelling at him. A man had to take what he could get in a tricky situation such as this.

But part of him almost wished she was shouting at him. The silence was getting to him. Rebecca had been unnaturally quiet since leaving the restaurant. She seemed distant somehow, as if she were deeply involved in her own thoughts and didn't have any intention of letting him know what those thoughts were about.

Kyle realized he didn't especially like the feeling of being out of contact with her. It made him realize how accustomed he had become to the vague, but pleasant sensation of being *in* contact with Rebecca. During the past ten days he had begun to experience the novelty of learning to communicate with a woman. Rebecca had seemed to understand him. Hell, Rebecca had loved him.

As they approached Harmony Valley, Kyle tried to lighten the atmosphere by playing tour guide. "This is fine country," he said. He was aware of a familiar sense of pleasure as he pointed out the lushness of the small valley and the spectacular mountain slopes that framed it. "Good grazing or farmland on the valley floor, and the full potential of the hillsides was never really exploited during the mining boom. No telling what's left up there in those hills. There's a wide creek that runs year-round."

"What did Alice Cork do out here all by herself for so many years?" Rebecca asked wonderingly as she surveyed the verdant scenery. It was the first time she had spoken since leaving the restaurant.

Kyle glanced at her out of the corner of his eye, trying to assess her mood. Rebecca's moods had never been difficult to read in the past. Now he found himself struggling to second-guess her. It made him uneasy.

"Alice farmed for the most part," Kyle said. "Ran a few cattle for a while and later some sheep. The stock was all sold off before she died. Guess she knew the end was coming. Alice always had a way of knowing things."

"What kind of things?"

Kyle shrugged. "I don't know how to explain it. She just seemed to be aware of certain matters. Like when babies were due, for instance. She was a sort of local midwife. Folks living out here can't always get to the hospital in time, especially if the weather's bad. Alice would get out of bed in the middle of snow storms and drive that old four-wheel-drive truck of hers to a rancher's house just in time to deliver a baby."

"Really?" Rebecca's eyes were suddenly bright with interest.

"Yeah. Really." Kyle gave her a laconic glance, pleased at having finally elicited some genuine attention from her. "The interesting part is that, half the time no one had to call her for help. She just showed up at the right moment. As if she knew exactly when things were scheduled to get serious. She was good with animals, too. The local vet used to consult with her on occasion." Kyle paused, remembering. "Once she saved a dog of mine."

"What happened?"

"Joker got real sick. The vet said he wouldn't make it and the best thing to do was put the dog to sleep. Dad said it was my decision but if it was up to him, he'd get a second opinion."

"Your dad suggested you take Joker to Alice?"

Kyle nodded. "And the vet agreed. Said it couldn't hurt. So I put poor Joker in the back of the truck and Dad and I drove out to see Alice. Dad warned me she might not let us in the driveway. She was known to greet Stockbridges and Ballards with a shotgun. But that day she let us drive right up to the front door. She walked out as if she'd been expecting us and just told Dad to carry Joker inside. Dad did it without saying a word. Alice told us to leave and we did."

"What happened to Joker?"

"We got a phone call from Alice five days later. She just said it was time to come get Joker and then she hung up the phone. Dad and I drove back out to her place and Joker came racing out of the house to greet us, good as new. Dad tried to pay Alice but she told him there were some things Stockbridge money couldn't buy. She kicked us out the door. I went back later to try to thank her for saving Joker's life but she wouldn't let me past the front gate."

"She sounds fascinating."

Kyle wasn't sure he liked the tone of open admiration. His eyes narrowed as he eased the Porsche onto the deeply grooved road that led to the old Cork house. "She was a stubborn, difficult, mean-tempered witch."

"You're a Stockbridge. Therefore, you're prejudiced."

Kyle shook his head. "Ask anyone."

"I'll make my own judgments. After all, she was my relative, even if I never heard of her." Rebecca leaned forward with sudden eagerness. "Is that the house?"

"That's it. Not much to look at." Alice took better care of the barn and her garden than she did of the house.

The ramshackle ranch house looked as if it would collapse in a strong wind. The weathered wood was gray with age and lack of paint. The porch roof sagged precariously.

Rebecca had the Porsche door open before Kyle had even turned off the ignition. Her fascination with Alice Cork and the old house was beginning to get to him. He'd never seen Rebecca act this way.

He got out of the car and followed her up the steps to the porch, watching as she withdrew a set of keys from her purse. He felt a strange chill of unease as she opened the door and went inside. This was forbidden territory. Forbidden, at least, to Stockbridges and Ballards. He felt as if he were trespassing—which was a damned fool thing to feel, considering that his right to this valley was stronger than anyone else's including Rebecca's.

Rebecca glanced over her shoulder, as if sensing his hesitation. "What's wrong?" she asked with a small frown.

"Nothing." Kyle was suddenly irritated with himself. He strode boldly into the house. "Alice Cork would have a fit if she could see me now. She never let me step foot in here. The day we brought Joker to her, she allowed Dad to carry him into the living room and put him down in front of the fire and that was it. I had to wait on the porch."

"Look at this place," Rebecca said softly. "It looks like something out of a museum of late nineteenth-century Americana." She studied the massive stone fireplace, the braided rug, the worn, hardwood floors and the old furnishings. "No modern appliances, no central heat. The only thing that looks reasonably new is the telephone."

"She needed a phone. People were always calling to ask for advice on how to handle the flu or a stomachache." Kyle felt a rush of subdued excitement as he strolled through the old house.

At last, after all these years, Harmony Valley was within reach. It was closer now than it had ever been to belonging to the owner of Flaming Luck Ranch. If his luck held, he would have it all, he told himself. There was no reason why both Rebecca and the valley should not wind up belonging to him. His confidence was returning rapidly.

"You can get that look out of your eye, Kyle."

Rebecca spoke from the other side of the living room. She was examining the faded chintz drapes. "This place is mine."

Her perception annoyed him. "And you belong to me," he reminded her curtly.

"No more than Alice belonged to your father or her mother belonged to your grandfather. It's interesting, isn't it, Kyle?"

"What's interesting?" he asked challengingly.

"How those women held out against both the Ballards and the Stockbridges. I feel as if a tradition has been passed on to me."

"Don't get any ideas," he warned, trying to squelch the flicker of panic he felt when she looked at him that way. "Besides, you didn't exactly hold out against a Stockbridge, if you'll recall," he added bluntly.

She shrugged. "A mistake, I admit. I didn't know about the family tradition at that point. Now I do."

Kyle closed the drawer of a bureau with a violent shove and shot Rebecca a quelling look. "Don't call our relationship a mistake, damn it. And don't start talking about family traditions. You didn't even know Alice Cork was family until yesterday."

"I'm sorry about never having met her," Rebecca said with genuine regret as she prowled through a desk. "I would like to have known her. She must have been a remarkable woman. I like this old house of hers."

Kyle decided intimidation was not going to

work. He wished he knew how to deal with Rebecca today. Her aloofness was making him increasingly wary. He had been so certain he would be able to handle her when she found out the truth—so sure he could control the situation without losing either the woman or the land. But everything was in danger of unraveling.

"Baby, be reasonable. This old place is dangerous. Portions of it could collapse at any moment. The only sensible thing to do is tear it down."

Rebecca glanced back at him. "And build a new house?"

Kyle looked at her and slowly shook his head. He glanced out the window at the beautiful mountain slopes. "You know what I'd do with this valley?"

"What?" Rebecca didn't move. She was watching him intently.

"I'd put in a first-class ski resort."

"A ski resort!" She seemed startled.

Kyle nodded. "I've been thinking about it for a long time. Harmony Valley would make a great ski area. The resort would bring new business and new life into these mountains. It would revitalize the area economically. If it was well planned, the resort could be used year-round. We get plenty of tourists driving through here in the summer. No reason they can't be persuaded to stop."

"That kind of development would take an enormous amount of financial backing," Rebecca observed. "Flaming Luck Enterprises couldn't do it alone. You'd need to bring in other investors."

Kyle braced one hand against the window, thinking about his dreams. "It could be done," he insisted.

"If I sell you the land," Rebecca retorted crisply. "I'll be perfectly honest with you, Kyle. Right now I have no idea what I'm going to do with Harmony Valley."

"Becky, you're a reasonable woman. Most of the time, at any rate. You know damned well there's nothing else you can do with this place except sell it. I can't see you living out here alone the way Alice did. You'd go crazy."

"Maybe. Maybe not." Rebecca opened another drawer in the old desk.

"Don't fight me on this, baby," Kyle coaxed softly. "Sell me the land and everything will go back to the way it was between us. You'll see. You were happy with me, Becky. Admit it."

"Ten days of living together is hardly long enough to produce an informed opinion on that subject," she said. "Look, there's an old book in here."

"You only lived with me for ten days, but you've worked for me for two months. That time counts, too, Becky. We've gotten to know each other. We also happen to be wild about each other in bed. We belong together. Once you get over being upset about this business with Harmony Valley, you'll realize I'm right. Give me a chance, Becky. You owe me that much. Sell me the land

and I'll prove that nothing has changed for us. Our relationship has nothing to do with this valley."

"It's a journal," Rebecca said softly. She was paying no attention to Kyle as she turned the old, leather-bound volume over and over in her hands. "Or a diary." She opened it. "Seems to be a record of farm business along with a lot of personal notes."

"Becky," Kyle said deliberately, sensing he had lost her attention again. "Forget that stupid journal. I'm trying to talk to you about the serious situation in which we find ourselves. It's important for couples to talk."

"Is it?" she asked vaguely, frowning over the journal.

"Well, of course it is," he exploded. "We're supposed to communicate. Talk out our problems. Every fog-brained shrink who decides to write a book says stuff like that."

"I didn't know you read that kind of stuff." Rebecca took one last glance around the small house. "And since when did you decide open communication between a man and a woman was such a hot idea? The only subject you've ever really opened up on with me was business."

"I like talking business with you," he shot back. "We understand each other. No reason we can't communicate on other subjects, too."

"Some other time, perhaps," she said politely. "I think I'm finished here for today, Kyle. Please take me back to the motel. I want to think about all this.''

Kyle recognized a stone wall when he ran straight into one. He backed off and tried another approach. ''You can stay at the ranch,'' he said nonchalantly as he walked toward the door. ''Plenty of room. I phoned the woman who cleans for me and warned her we'd be there tonight. She promised to stock the refrigerator and change the bed.''

''I'm staying at the motel, Kyle.''

He made a grab for his patience. ''There are four bedrooms at the Flaming Luck. You can take your pick,'' he said harshly. The thought of her sleeping without him was hard to swallow, but he told himself he had to handle her carefully now.

''I'm staying at the motel,'' Rebecca repeated. The journal was tucked under her arm as she went outside onto the porch.

''Becky, it's not even three o'clock. Come on over to the Flaming Luck with me. I'd like to show you the place.''

''I can't fit the tour into my schedule this afternoon, I'm afraid.''

''What are you going to do? Sit around that dump of a motel all afternoon and evening? You'll be bored to tears.''

''No, I won't. I'm going to read Alice's journal. Catch up on a little local history.''

''Alice Cork's version of history?''

''Why not?''

"Don't you think it will be slightly biased?" he asked roughly.

"History is always biased," she informed him mildly. "That's because there are only two kinds—the winner's version, and the loser's version. The trick is to know which version you're reading."

"Do you think Alice was on the winning side?"

"In this particular battle there don't appear to have been any real winners. Maybe there never will be." Rebecca walked away.

"There might not have been any winners, but there's definitely a right side and a wrong side in this particular battle," Kyle yelled after her.

"In that case it looks like I'm on the side of the Cork women."

"That happens to be the wrong side!"

"That's a matter of opinion."

Kyle almost leaped after her to demand that she have dinner with him. After that he could coax her out to the house. He was sure of it. All he needed was a little time.

But a shrewd jolt of common sense held him back. He would take her back into town and give her a night by herself in that flea trap of a motel. By tomorrow morning she would welcome the sight of him. When he invited her out for breakfast, she would probably trip over her own feet accepting.

A smart man knew when to bide his time.

SIX

Rebecca got up at dawn the next morning. She had stayed awake much of the night pouring over Alice Cork's fascinating, insightful journal. Sleeping in should have sounded like a good idea but Rebecca was feeling too restless. She wanted to go back out to the Cork place. She needed to get more of a feel for Alice and her mother.

It was still dark when Rebecca pulled out of the motel parking lot, but the first rays of light were creeping over the mountain peaks when she reached the old Cork house. She parked her car in the driveway, picked up the journal she had brought with her and went inside.

Wooden floorboards creaked and something small with a tail scuttled furiously out of the way as Rebecca opened the door. The house seemed to groan with the accumulated weight of years of hard work and aloneness. Alice Cork had been strangely content here in her later years, Rebecca had learned. But the early years were a different matter. The loss of her parents and then the

trauma of falling hopelessly in love with Glen
Ballard's father had taken their toll on Alice. Losing the baby had been another heavy blow. She
had sensed somehow that she would never have
another child. Kyle was right. Alice Cork had a
way of knowing things.

Rebecca walked through the house as she had
yesterday afternoon, pausing to examine a faded
photo, a handmade quilt, an old harness that
needed repair.

Finally she sat down at the scarred oak table
and opened the journal.

*Old Hank at the store told me today that Martha
Stockbridge has left Cale. No one is surprised. It was
only a matter of time. Poor little Martha was no match
for that black-haired devil she married. I knew the first
time I saw her that she would never be able to cope with
the Stockbridge temper. She was too timid and too
young to handle Cale. He must have terrified her often
during the three years they've been married. Everyone
says the Stockbridge luck doesn't do much good with
women. But I know it isn't a matter of luck. The Stockbridge men, like the Ballard men, are incapable of loving anyone or anything except their land.*

Rebecca glanced up from her reading, thinking
about the young, timid woman who had been
Kyle's mother. Then she went back to the next
paragraph in the journal.

*The boy is only two. He won't remember his mother.
That's a pity because it means there will be no gentleness in his life. No softness. Nothing to counter Cale's
influence. But no one can blame Martha for leaving.*

What woman could stand against the Stockbridge tem-
per and ruthlessness? Another generation of hard, ar-
rogant Stockbridges has been hatched. I saw little Kyle
with his father in town the other day. He looks exactly
like Cale, right down to those terrifying green eyes. I
see no trace of Martha in him. The Stockbridge men are
a dynasty of dragons, and they breed true.

A dynasty of dragons. Rebecca almost smiled,
remembering how Kyle's staff often termed him a
dragon. It must be the green eyes and all that nonsense about breathing fire, she decided. But Alice
had been wrong on one count. Neither dragons
nor anyone else bred photocopies of themselves.

She didn't know what Cale had been like, certainly not a lovable man from all accounts. But
Kyle wasn't an exact duplicate of his parent. She
knew him well enough to know that. After all, she
had fallen in love with him. By definition, that
made him lovable.

Of course, that might also make her a woman
of questionable intelligence, she reminded herself.

The sound of hoofbeats caught her attention.
Startled, Rebecca closed the journal and went to
the door. She opened it to find a vision from the
past. It made her wonder if Harmony Valley existed in some sort of time warp.

Kyle was approaching astride a high black stallion. The big horse moved at an easy canter, and
Kyle rode as if the animal were a part of him. A
small bay mare on a leading rope loped along-
side. The mare was saddled and bridled.

Rebecca watched the man and his horses ride in out of the dawn, and something within her stirred. Kyle was born for this landscape, she thought. This was where he was at home.

"Morning, Becky," Kyle said easily as he rode the black stallion right up to the front of the porch. Saddle leather creaked and the big black shook his head, blowing softly. Kyle leaned forward and rested his forearm on the horn. His green eyes gleamed at her from the shadow of the Stetson. "When you didn't answer the phone in your motel room, I thought I might find you here. I came to take you to breakfast."

Rebecca folded her arms and leaned against the door post. "We're going to ride into town?"

Kyle shook his head. "No. Up into the mountains above this valley." He patted a bulging saddlebag. "I've got biscuits and coffee right here."

"What makes you think I can ride?"

"Instinct." He smiled fleetingly. "But if you can't there's nothing to worry about. Anyone could stay up on Athena here." He nodded at the bay mare who was nuzzling the ragged bushes in front of the porch. "She's as gentle as a lamb."

"What about your horse?" she asked curiously.

Kyle patted the black's arching neck. The horse stamped a foot. "You want to tackle old Tulip?" he asked, brows rising.

"Tulip!" Rebecca smiled in spite of herself. "He doesn't look much like a Tulip."

"He wasn't named for his looks. He was named for his personality."

"I see. He's sweet natured and delicate, I take it."

"Fact is, he's a real bastard most of the time," Kyle confided equably. "Especially when he hasn't been ridden in a while."

"The two of you seem to get along well."

"We understand each other."

"Two of a kind?" Rebecca murmured.

Kyle straightened in the saddle. "Let's go," he said evenly.

He hadn't liked that. Rebecca said nothing for a moment, considering her options. One was to stay here and go hungry. The other was to go horseback riding in the early-morning light and share biscuits and coffee with Kyle.

No contest.

Rebecca pocketed the keys to Alice Cork's house, walked down the steps without a word and slipped a foot into Athena's stirrup. She picked up the reins as Kyle detached the lead.

"You can ride, can't you?" Kyle asked quizzically.

"I can manage."

"I thought so," he muttered under his breath. "You always do. You are one managing female." He nudged Tulip, and the big black moved forward eagerly.

Athena followed and within minutes they were moving across the meadow behind Alice Cork's house, heading for the nearby hills. Rebecca took a deep breath of the fresh morning air and settled into the mare's comfortable stride. The sunlight lancing into Harmony Valley was incredibly beautiful. It danced off distant peaks and glinted on the water in the wide creek. Wild flowers opened their petals to the warmth with the eagerness of young lovers.

Kyle rode in silence, glancing over his shoulder once in a while to make certain Rebecca was keeping up with him. There was distant approval in his eyes as he saw how easily she rode.

When he finally called a halt they were high on a ridge overlooking the valley. Kyle swung off Tulip and dropped the reins casually onto the ground. Tulip stood as if anchored to stone. Rebecca followed suit. She winced as she slid out of the saddle.

"I'm going to feel this tomorrow," she complained. "I haven't ridden in several years."

Kyle grinned. "I've got something to take your mind off your troubles." He removed a thermos from the saddlebags. "Coffee."

"I could use a cup." Rebecca walked over to a large boulder and scrambled up on top of it to see the view. Harmony Valley was stretched out before her in all its early-morning glory.

"Quite a sight up here at his time of day, isn't it?" Kyle climbed up to stand beside Rebecca. He handed her a cup of coffee and a biscuit. He sipped from his own mug.

"Very beautiful."

"I used to ride over here sometimes when I was a kid. I'd stand up here on this rock and tell myself that everything down there in the valley was someday going to be mine. I decided I was the Stockbridge who was finally going to get this valley once and for all."

"You were pretty arrogant for a kid, weren't you?"

Kyle shrugged. "I knew what I wanted. That's all."

"Why is it so important for you to have Harmony Valley?"

Kyle looked out over the valley, his eyes reflective. "Because."

"That's a compelling reason, all right," Rebecca observed sarcastically.

Kyle turned his head to look at her. "When a man wants something, when he knows in his gut it belongs to him, that's all the reason he has to have to pursue it. It's only women who insist on dissecting a perfectly normal desire, trying to figure out what makes it exist."

Rebecca sat down on the cold granite and folded her legs tailor fashion. The coffee cup was comforting and warm in her hands. "I think there's room for disagreement on that subject, but I don't plan to get into it now. Did you ever bring your wife up here? Or Darla?"

Kyle didn't move for a long moment. Then he slowly lowered himself into a sitting position beside Rebecca. "There's no point rehashing the past, Becky."

"I'd like to talk about it."

"Why?" He sounded aggressive, as if he were bracing himself for battle. "You already know I haven't got much of a track record in the marriage department."

"Tell me about your ex-wife," Rebecca insisted gently. "According to Alice's journal, her name was Heather."

He gave her a startled glance. "Alice wrote about my marriage?"

"Alice kept close track of the Ballards and the Stockbridges," Rebecca explained. "You might say that keeping track of the doings of Ballards and Stockbridges was a hobby of hers. She was probably operating on the principle of knowing one's enemy."

Kyle grunted his disapproval. He looked out over the valley. When he finally started speaking, his voice was clipped and unemotional, as if he had distanced himself from the circumstances surrounding his first marriage.

"Heather was a little slip of a thing. Pretty, blond, big blue eyes. I met her in college. Couldn't wait to bring her home to show her the ranch and have her meet Dad. Dad took one look at her and told me she was too soft for me. No staying power, he said. Too much like my mother. I explained to him that Heather was gentle and delicate. She needed protecting and I wanted to protect her. I was going through an idealistic phase, I guess."

"What did your father say?"

"He asked me who was going to protect her from me." Kyle bit down savagely on a biscuit.

Rebecca studied his hard profile. "You married her over your father's objections?"

"He didn't object, exactly. He just predicted the whole thing was going to be a disaster. Said I was too young to know what I needed in a woman. He was right. To make a long story short, times started getting rough in the cattle business. Then Dad died. I dropped out of college in my senior year to go to work. Heather began to cry a lot."

"That must have gone over real big with you," Rebecca murmured. Kyle was not the kind of man who would have a lot of patience with sobbing females.

"Things weren't working out the way she had planned," Kyle explained soberly. "Money was short. She was young and wanted to have some fun. I was working long hours trying to hold on to the ranch land. I didn't have the time or inclination to indulge her childish whims." He shook his head. "I guess I got impatient. Lost my temper a few times. Told her it would greatly help the family finances if she went to work. She cried some more. I yelled at her some more. Things went downhill rapidly. Then I made the mistake of talking about babies."

"Babies?"

"Yeah. I thought maybe a baby would settle her down. Besides, Stockbridges always have sons, and I figured it was time to have one of my own."

"And she didn't agree?"

"Hell, no. She panicked. Said she was too

young to start a family. There wasn't enough money. She wanted to have some fun before she got tied down to a baby, et cetera, et cetera. We had one last big fight during which I really lost my temper, and she ran home to her parents. She filed for divorce the next day."

"Did you love her?"

Kyle rubbed his jaw. "I thought I did in the beginning. As I said, I was in my idealistic phase. But whatever I felt for her at the start of the marriage was long gone by the time the divorce papers arrived. Fact is, it was kind of a relief when it was all over."

"You might be interested to know that Alice predicted the same ending to your marriage that your father did. She thought Heather would collapse like a hothouse rose in the first major storm."

"Sounds like everyone was a hell of a lot more farsighted than I was," Kyle growled.

"Alice saw things, all right. Did you know she thought of Stockbridges as a nest of fire-breathing dragons?"

Kyle winced. "Alice called me a dragon?"

"She said you were the latest in a long line of green-eyed monsters."

"Is that right?" he demanded with familiar aggression. "What did she call the Ballard family?"

Rebecca's mouth curved slightly as she remembered that section of the journal. "A clan of sorcerers. She thought they used their charms to seduce and destroy others."

"Alice may have hit the nail on the head with that one." Kyle looked vaguely placated.

"She may have hit the nail on the head with both observations," Rebecca retorted. "She had a lot of time to consider the various aspects of the two families. Tell me about your engagement."

Kyle poured himself another cup of coffee. "You just won't quit, will you?"

"No."

"Well, since you've heard about the marriage, I guess there's no reason not to tell you about Darla. Not all that much to tell, really. Darla is a nice person. I'd always liked her in a vague kind of way. The way a man would like a younger sister, I guess. We lost track of each other for a few years after college. But when I met her again in Denver four years ago, I took one look at her and knew she was just what I needed. She wasn't the type of woman who would give me any trouble. She wasn't after my money. She wouldn't be too demanding. She would make a good hostess. She had no objections to giving me a son. To top it all off, she was pretty. What more could a man want?"

"In other words, you were going through a practical phase."

"Probably." Kyle capped the thermos and sat staring broodingly out over Harmony Valley. "But I managed to screw up that relationship, too."

"Your temper again?" Rebecca asked softly.

Kyle drummed his fingers on the granite. "That

was part of it, I think. But not all. By the time I met Darla, I had learned to control my temper."

"Really?" Rebecca let her skepticism show in her voice.

Kyle shot her an aggrieved glance. "It's true. I'm a hell of a lot mellower now than I was in my younger days. People do change, you know."

"I've certainly seen lots of examples of the new, mellow Kyle Stockbridge," Rebecca pointed out meaningfully.

"Damn it. I've never lost my temper with you, Becky."

Rebecca slid him a sidelong glance and realized he was telling the truth. From his point of view, he'd never lost his temper with her. The moments of impatience and minor annoyance she had witnessed during the past couple of months clearly did not count as far as he was concerned. The realization that she'd never been the victim of one of Kyle's full-blown rages was somewhat unnerving. She wondered just how bad the storm could be.

"Who ended the engagement?" Rebecca asked quietly. "You or Darla?"

"Glen Ballard ended the engagement." Kyle said shortly. "Darla didn't have the guts to tell me herself."

Rebecca sighed. "I can just imagine that little scene."

"I doubt it." Kyle turned to look at her, his expression one of challenge. "Okay. You've heard all the sordid details. Now you know just how lousy my track record is when it comes to marriage. It's a typical Stockbridge record. My father didn't do any better and neither did my grandfather. My grandmother didn't leave because in those days people just didn't get divorced. But I remember how sullen and quiet she was all the time. She was obviously one miserable female and she didn't care who knew it. When I was eight, she told me she envied my mother for having the courage to walk out."

"What a pleasant old lady," Rebecca said grimly. Just the sort of sweet, grandmotherly type a motherless boy needed, she thought with sarcasm. But then she realized how trapped and bitter the woman must have been. "Sounds to me like the Stockbridge men do a lousy job of picking their women."

"Most people would say it wouldn't matter what woman a Stockbridge picked. The marriage would be doomed right from the start," Kyle said quietly.

"You mean because of the infamous Stockbridge temper?"

Kyle shrugged. "I guess you could say the Stockbridge men have trouble relating."

"Don't lump yourself in with your father and grandfather, Kyle. You're not a reincarnation of either of them. You're you. You can do whatever you want to do. You don't have to repeat their mistakes."

"Thank you, Miss Therapist." Kyle picked up a shard of granite and tossed it out over the edge of the ridge. "So much for confession time. Are you satisfied?"

"No. But we can worry about that later." She smiled brightly when he shot her a glowering look. "According to Alice Cork's journal, the Ballards haven't had a particularly admirable record with women, either. She said the Ballard men were all womanizers. Seducers of innocent females. Glen's mother and grandmother apparently suffered in tearful silence for the most part while their husbands chased anything in skirts."

"The famous Ballard charm," Kyle said scathingly.

"Is Glen Ballard like that?"

"Wouldn't surprise me. I warned Darla about that but she wouldn't listen. She was convinced Glen was different."

"Come on, Kyle. Tell me the truth. Is Glen like his father or grandfather?" Rebecca persisted.

"How the hell should I know? I don't keep track of Ballard's affairs." Kyle leaned back on his elbows and scowled at Rebecca.

"In a small community like this everyone can't help but keep track of other people's affairs. You'd hear gossip if Glen Ballard was running around on his wife."

"Okay, okay. So maybe Glen isn't as bad as his old man in that department."

"Aha! You mean he's been faithful to Darla?"

"Far as I know," Kyle admitted grudgingly. "Let's change the subject. The last thing I want to talk about this morning is Glen Ballard."

"What do you want to talk about?"

"You."

"What about me?"

"You're thirty years old, and you're the sexiest woman I've ever met," he said bluntly. "So why weren't you married long before I met you?"

Rebecca was taken aback. "The sexiest woman you've ever met?" she asked in amazement.

"You can drive me crazy just going through the weekly report in my office," he said flatly. "You walk through the door on Friday morning with your little clipboard in your hand, and the first thing I want to do is tear off your clothes and lay you down on the office sofa."

She turned pink as she heard the ring of sincerity in his voice. She had to remind herself that Kyle's desire for Harmony Valley was the strongest motivating force in his life. It could lead him to make a lot of wild, exciting statements that sounded quite sincere. In other words, he might be lying through his teeth.

Still, the thought of being able to drive him nuts with the weekly report was a dangerously thrilling one. Until she had met Kyle, Rebecca had never thought of herself as a particularly sensual woman. One of the things he had given her, she realized suddenly, was a new level of confidence in her own sensuality.

"Why, Becky?" he asked again when she remained silent.

"There was a man once," she admitted slowly. "About four years ago. Everything seemed right.

We were both getting established in our careers. Both on the way up. We laughed a lot together. We enjoyed doing the same things. We talked a lot. About old films. Good food. Cats. We were in love."

Kyle seized another chunk of granite and sent it hurling out into the valley below. "Go on," he said roughly. "What happened to this paragon of modern manhood?"

"We were together for about a year and a half. We were planning a wedding. Trying to set a date that wouldn't conflict with my schedule or his. I should have realized something was wrong when we couldn't seem to pick a date that fit his time-table. It took me quite a while to realize he had gotten cold feet and was looking for a way out."

"Why did he want out?"

Rebecca folded her arms on top of her updrawn knees. "He said I overpowered him. That I was too assertive. Too aggressive for a woman. Too independent. Too managing. My biggest fault, I think, was that I was making as much money as he was. That bothered him. Really bothered him."

"Guy sounds like a real jerk."

"I eventually came to that conclusion myself."

"What happened to him?"

Rebecca smiled briefly. "He married some little harebrained ex-cheerleader who happened to be his secretary."

"Sounds like he got what he deserved," Kyle scoffed.

"Goes to show that everybody is capable of

making a few mistakes in the relationship department," Rebecca mused. "You don't have a monopoly on the ability."

"Probably not." Kyle stared out over the valley from beneath hooded eyes. "But the Stockbridges tend to make more than their share of mistakes in that field and I've sure as hell done my part to live up to the family tradition."

"Do you realize that this is the first really meaningful discussion about our pasts that we've ever had?" Rebecca asked.

"It wasn't a discussion I ever wanted to have."

"I know. Why?"

"I figured it would scare you off," he said frankly. "I didn't want you summing me up as a two-time loser."

"You're not a loser." Rebecca got to her feet and dusted off the seat of her jeans. "You just never met the right woman. That's all." She started back toward the horses.

"Becky, wait…" Kyle leaped to his feet and followed. "What do you mean, I never met the right woman?"

"It's simple," she explained as she picked up Athena's reins. "So far you've tried twice, right? You managed to choose a wimp the first time around, and the second time you went for the comfortable type you figured wouldn't give you any trouble." She swung herself up into the saddle. "You made some mistakes, and now you're gun-shy. That's understandable. Obviously the choice of a bride is too complicated to be left in your hands. The Stockbridge men apparently need help in making such an important decision.''

Rebecca turned Athena and started down the hillside. Kyle watched her for a minute, trying to decide how to take her last words. He felt confused and disoriented. He shouldn't have allowed Rebecca to draw him into a discussion of his past. He had long ago determined not to tell her about his record of failure with women.

But she hadn't seemed all that upset by the story of his disastrous marriage and broken engagement. In fact, she had taken the tale in stride.

He worried on one hand that her casual attitude stemmed from her loss of interest in him. Maybe she simply didn't care any longer. But there was another possibility, he told himself. Maybe Rebecca just wasn't as alarmed as he had feared she would be by those grim details of his past. Maybe she didn't consider them all that terrible, after all.

Kyle vaulted onto Tulip's back and followed Rebecca down the hill. He wasn't about to give up. The small flame of hope that still flickered within him wouldn't be extinguished easily. Rebecca was the one woman in the world for him. He had to get her back.

She had taught him what it meant not to be alone.

Rebecca spent the rest of the morning poking around Alice Cork's house and barn. Kyle tried to coax her into coming back to his house for lunch, but Rebecca firmly resisted. He left her alone eventually, jamming his hat down over his eyes and stalking off to mount Tulip. The two horses cantered away in a cloud of dust. Rebecca watched them leave, and then she went back to work.

By midafternoon, she was hungry. She drove back to town and parked her car in the motel lot. Then she walked across the street to buy sandwich makings. She wasn't in the mood for another hamburger at the small café.

The eager curiosity on the face of the grocery-store owner didn't surprise her. She was getting accustomed to the interest everyone in the little community was taking in her.

"You been out to the Cork place yet?" the elderly man asked cheerfully. "Not exactly a mansion, is it? Old Alice took good care of her animals, but toward the end she let the house and barn go. Probably didn't feel up to the work. The wife and I—I'm Herb Crocket, by the way—we took a load of groceries out to her coupla times a week when she got to the point where she couldn't make it into town. Ethel, that's my wife, tried to tidy things up a bit, but Alice didn't want her fussing. Alice always was real independent. Just like her ma."

"I went out this morning," Rebecca said as she chose a loaf of bread.

"Pretty little valley, isn't it?" Herb asked, his eyes shrewd. "If you want my advice, I'd sell it quick. You don't want to be in the middle when the war heats up between Ballard and Stockbridge. Take the best offer and duck. But don't look for a buyer from these parts. Everyone here knows the situation. You'll need to sell it to some fool from Denver or maybe a Californian."

"The Ballards and the Stockbridges certainly have quite a reputation in this area," Rebecca observed mildly.

"They deserve it," Herb informed her with a certain relish. "Kyle and Glen have been wrangling since kindergarten. Come by that attitude honestly, though. Their pappies were just as bad and the granddaddies were worse. Story is that the grandaddies actually took shots at each other. Folks got themselves killed from time to time over that valley."

"While the townspeople took bets?" Rebecca asked bluntly.

Herb Crocket blinked and then chuckled. "I won't say that the warfare hasn't provided a few interesting moments down through the years. I made five bucks off Stockbridge once, myself. He and Ballard got into it down by the river on the way home from a high-school dance. Ballard wound up in the water. Me and Tim Murphy was drivin' by in my car, and we saw the whole thing. Murphy bet on Ballard, and I took Stockbridge."

Rebecca had a mental image of a bunch of on-lookers standing around placing bets while the town's two bad boys went at it.

"Now, Herb, don't you be givin' Miss Wade a

bad impression," said a gray-haired, bespecta-
cled woman from the rear of the store. She came
forward between two aisles of canned goods, her
ample bosom covered by a large white apron. She
smiled with sunny good humor at Rebecca.
"Don't pay him any attention. For years there's
been way too many of them like Herb here that
didn't mind enjoying the show those two families
have always put on."

"Ain't my fault that feud has kept going for
three generations, Ethel," Herb grumbled.

"Should have been stopped years ago," Ethel
opined. She peered at Rebecca. "If you ask me, a
smart woman could have done something about
that situation somewhere along the line. But Ballards and Stockbridges never did tend to marry
smart. Leastways, they didn't before young Glen
married little Darla. Always did like Darla. Sensible woman. Good head on her shoulders. Glen's
calmed down a lot since the two of them got
hitched. She's a good influence on him."

"Ain't no woman born who could manage either a Ballard or a Stockbridge when it comes to
Harmony Valley," Herb declared. "Ballards and
Stockbridges have always been plumb crazy
when it comes to that land."

The bells on the door jingled merrily just as Rebecca put her selections on the counter. A lanky-
looking teenager stuck his head inside the store.
He was grinning with gleeful anticipation.

"Word is, anyone who wants to see Ballard and
Stockbridge go at it better get down to Cully's

Tavern," he announced. "Stockbridge is in there shootin' pool, I hear, and Ballard just drove up. Bound to be some fireworks."

"Here we go again," Ethel Crocket said with a sigh.

"Yup," said Herb, looking enthusiastic.

"Nope," said Rebecca very quietly and very firmly. "Excuse me, Herb. I'll be back to pick these things up later."

"Where are you going?" Herb asked in astonishment.

"To see the local sights. Care to direct me to Cully's Tavern?"

Herb stared at her. "Outside to the left. Half a block down. Can't miss it. But you shouldn't be headin' there, ma'am. It ain't exactly the sort of place a nice woman like yourself would feel comfortable in, if you know what I mean."

"Thank you," said Rebecca. She headed for the door.

"Oh, Lordy," said Ethel. "Herb, you go after her. She doesn't know what she's getting into."

"What the heck am I supposed to do?" Herb demanded. But he was reluctantly untying his apron.

Rebecca paid no attention. She walked outside and turned left. Herb was right. It was impossible to miss Cully's Tavern. Half a block down from the grocery store she stopped in front of a neon sign advertising beer and pool. The view through the narrow little windows was hampered by aging red curtains that hadn't been cleaned in years.

A battered metal plate over the door warned minors they were not allowed across the threshold. There was a grimy, laid-back, males-only atmosphere about the place that warned Rebecca what she would find inside.

She ignored the warning and pushed open the door. A cloud of stale cigarette smoke, alcohol fumes and masculine tension greeted her. Through the haze she could make out a collection of colorful beer logos decorating the walls.

The jukebox was halfway through a song about cheating men and faithful, crying women. Several males dressed in jeans and work clothes slouched on shabby bar stools. They were sipping beer and watching the pool table with riveted attention.

Everyone at the bar looked over as Rebecca walked into the tavern. A rumble of questioning surprise went through the sleazy room. She scanned the row of faces at the bar and then looked over at the pool table.

Kyle was leaning over the table, cue poised for a shot. The planes of his face were harshly illuminated by the triangle of light that shone down on the table. An intricate series of balls was lined up on the green felt.

A tall, strikingly handsome man with copper-colored hair was lounging nearby. He was watching Kyle line up the shot with the same attention he would probably have given a rattlesnake.

"I've got a proposition for you, Stockbridge," the red-haired man said in a drawling western accent. "One of us buys out the woman. Once we get her out of the picture, you and I can play a game of pool for the land."

"Forget it, Ballard." Kyle readjusted his aim.

"You always were a coward when it came to taking a risk. Guess you haven't changed much over the years. Sort of a Stockbridge characteristic."

"I can take a risk," Kyle retorted smoothly. "But I'll admit I prefer the calculated kind. I leave the damned fool kind of risks to Ballards."

"Just like you leave the women to us?" Ballard retorted easily.

"Go to hell, Ballard. I'm busy." Kyle loosed the pool cue. The shot was right on target. A ball dropped into the pocket. Kyle stood up and walked around the table, sizing up his next shot.

He leaned down to check his aim and caught sight of Rebecca. His gaze flew to her face. "What the devil are you doing here, Becky?"

"Soaking up a little local atmosphere." She stepped forward through the smoky haze and smiled at the red-haired man. "You, I take it, are Glen Ballard?"

"I am." Ballard straightened up and tipped his wide-brimmed western hat in an old-fashioned gesture. The taunting look left his eyes as he studied her. A slow smile curved his mouth. "And you must be Miss Rebecca Wade."

She inclined her head. "I'm afraid so."

"Becky, this is no place for you." Kyle dropped his pool cue on the table and came around the corner to grab her arm. "For Pete's sake, don't you know any better than to wander into a tavern? This isn't exactly a cocktail-and-sushi bar."

"I figured that out right after I opened the door."

"Miss Wade is safe enough in here," Glen Ballard said with soft challenge. "I'll protect her myself, if need be."

"The hell you will. Touch her and I'll feed you that pool cue."

"Kyle, please," Rebecca interrupted quickly. "Don't be an idiot."

"That's good advice. You ought to pay attention to the lady, Stockbridge." Ballard grinned wickedly. "'Course, that's probably tough advice for a Stockbridge to take." He looked at Rebecca. "Stockbridges just naturally tend to make idiots of themselves," he confided. "It's in the blood."

"Shut up, Ballard."

"Now why should I, Stockbridge?"

"Gentlemen, please." Rebecca said very firmly. She sensed the gathering excitement in the room. The men at the bar were edging closer. She thought she saw money being put on the counter and she knew it wasn't to pay for drinks. It was time to take charge of the situation. "There seems to be a misunderstanding here."

Neither man was paying any attention to her now.

"I said," Rebecca repeated in a louder voice, "there appears to be a misunderstanding here." She turned to face the crowd. "Instead of providing a show for you all today, Mr. Ballard and Mr.

Stockbridge would like to buy a round of drinks for everyone."

"Get out of here, Becky." Kyle was eyeing his opponent. "I'll be out as soon as I teach Ballard a few manners."

"I'll send him out to you minus a few basic parts, ma'am. I'm not sure he'll be much use to you after I get finished with him. But, then, Stockbridges have never been much use to anyone," Ballard said.

"I'm afraid I'm not making myself clear," Rebecca said coolly. "You will both cease and desist from this childish behavior at once. And then you will fork over enough cash to buy everyone in here a drink. If you don't, I will deed Harmony Valley over to one of those crazy religious cults that has its members out soliciting in airports. I understand they're always looking for places to build their communes."

"Don't be ridiculous, Becky." Kyle muttered.

"You know very well that I am seldom ridiculous. I mean every word I say. You both have sixty seconds to make up your minds."

Kyle swore and looked at Ballard. "I hate to say it, but she probably means it. I do know her. Unless you want this town filled with a bunch of weirdos and their gurus, you'd better do as she says." He fished his wallet out of his back pocket, walked over to the bar and put down several bills.

Ballard watched in astonishment. Then he looked at Rebecca's face as if seeing her for the first time. Something he saw there must have convinced him the threat was real. Thoughtfully he followed Kyle over to the bar and put down a stack of bills.

Rebecca was keenly aware of the stunned silence behind her as she turned and strode out of the tavern. She didn't need to look over her shoulder to know that Kyle and Glen were following her.

SEVEN

"So you're the new owner of Harmony Valley," Glen Ballard said as he trailed after Rebecca who was heading back toward the grocery store. "I'll tell you straight, ma'am, you aren't quite what I expected. Bet you weren't what Stockbridge here was expecting, either. Hey, here comes Herb. What's up, Herb? You look agitated."

Herb Crocket came to an awkward halt in front of Rebecca. He looked from her composed face to the scowling faces of the two men following at her heels. "Everything okay, Miss Wade?" he asked uneasily.

"Everything is just fine, Herb. Kyle and Glen just did their charitable deed for the day. They bought a round of drinks for everyone in Cully's Tavern. If you hurry, you might get a beer on the house."

"They chipped in together to buy a round of drinks? I don't believe it." Herb stared harder at Kyle and Glen. "Must be some mistake. I thought there was gonna be a..." He broke off quickly as the two men behind Rebecca fixed him with quelling stares.

"You thought there was going to be a fight?" Rebecca smiled politely. "Not today. Mr. Ballard and Mr. Stockbridge are going to behave themselves today. Aren't you, gentlemen?"

Kyle braced one hand against the nearest wall and bunched the other one into a fist at his hip. "This isn't funny, Becky."

"You can say that again," Glen Ballard muttered.

Herb looked from one man to the other with a dazed expression. "What isn't funny?" he finally asked.

"I've explained to both Mr. Ballard and Mr. Stockbridge that if either of them gets into a brawl this afternoon, I will be turning Harmony Valley over to a tribe of cultists. As you can see, Mr. Ballard and Mr. Stockbridge appear to be able to agree on a few things, one of which is that they don't want Harmony Valley going to a bunch of strange people in purple togas."

"Purple togas?" Herb Crocket looked more confused than ever.

"Run along to Cully's, Herb." Kyle looked bored. "Someone down there can explain the joke."

"I think I'll do that." Herb stepped around Rebecca and her entourage. "Your groceries are waiting for you, Miss Wade," he called back over his shoulder.

"Thank you, Herb." She resumed her determined stride toward the store. Both Glen and Kyle fell into step behind her again.

Neither said a word as she collected her sack of groceries from an astounded-looking Ethel and headed back across the street toward the motel.

Glen Ballard finally spoke up as he realized she was about to let herself into her room without another word to either of the two men who had been shadowing her like wary wolves.

"Miss Wade," Glen said, shedding some of the western twang in favor of a more businesslike tone, "I'd like to talk to you."

"Would you?" She turned on the step and eyed the two men assessingly. The difference between Glen Ballard and Kyle Stockbridge was the difference between night and day. They were clearly opposites. If Kyle was a man of dark, brooding shadows, it was fair to say that his counterpart was full of sunlight and roguish charm. It took a while to get to know Kyle well enough to figure out if you could ever like him, but Glen was the kind of person everyone responded positively to on sight. Unless of course one knew why he was turning on the charm.

"I certainly would," Glen said easily. "But my wife never allows me to talk business before dinner. She claims its bad for the stomach. Darla likes to fuss over me, and I'll be the first to admit I like being fussed over. She's the reason I'm here, by the way."

"Perhaps you'd better explain."

Glen's engaging smile brightened by a few

thousand watts. "I'm getting ahead of myself. Guess I'd better start from scratch." He executed a small, amusing bow. "Glen Ballard at your service, ma'am. My wife, Darla, and I got word you were in town. We wondered if you'd care to join us for a little get-together we had planned for this evening. Just a casual barbecue for a few of the neighbors. From all accounts, you definitely qualify as a new neighbor. Like to meet a few of the local folks?"

Meeting the neighbors sounded fine as far as it went. But Rebecca experienced a very odd sensation at the thought of socializing with the woman who had once been engaged to Kyle. Still, sooner or later she knew she was going to have to deal with the Ballards. A casual barbecue might be the easiest way to feel out the situation.

"That sounds wonderful," she said politely. "I accept."

Kyle swore. "Don't be a fool, Becky. I thought you were smart enough not to fall for the snake oil and greasy charm."

"Why don't you let the little lady make up her own mind, Stockbridge? You've had your chance with her. Kept her tucked away out of sight for over two months, from what I hear."

"The *little lady* makes her own choices," Kyle grated. "And she chose to stay with me for the past couple of months."

"Maybe that's because she didn't know why you were keeping such a close eye on her, hmmm?"

"The *little lady*," Rebecca broke in deliberately, "has no intention of listening to this kind of garbage on her own doorstep. If you will excuse me, I'm going to make myself a snack."

"My apologies, Miss Wade," Glen Ballard said with quick, apparently genuine contrition. "Didn't mean to upset you. Don't pay any attention to Stockbridge or me. We can't be in the same room together for more than five minutes without wrangling. It's in the blood, you know. Our daddies and granddaddies were the same way."

Kyle shot Glen a savage glance. "Don't let him charm you, Becky. He's good at it, I'll admit. But it's all fake. He'll smile like that while he's taking you for everything you've got."

"Miss Wade appears to be an intelligent woman. I expect she can tell the real thing from the fake when she sees it," Glen Ballard said gently. "Lord knows she's had long enough to figure out which category you fit into. Why don't you stand aside and give her a fair chance to get to know me?"

"I don't plan to stand aside for you or anyone else, Ballard."

"Why not?" Glen asked. "You ought to be used to it. You've had to stand aside in the past once or twice."

"Not for anything that mattered," Kyle said bluntly.

Rebecca saw the dangerous gleam in Kyle's eyes and a sinking feeling hit her. Glen must have been referring to the time he had married Kyle's fiancée, Darla. It was obvious from the expression on Kyle's face that the past was far from dead. She wondered how big a torch Kyle was carrying for the other woman.

"Listen, you sonofa…" Ballard began ominously.

"Excuse me," Rebecca interrupted crisply. "I've got better things to do than listen to this. Kindly remember my threat. I do not threaten lightly." She slammed the door hard enough to alarm anyone who happened to be in the neighboring room.

"I'll pick you up in an hour, Miss Wade," Glen yelled cheerfully through the door.

"Don't bother. I'll find my own way out to your place."

"If that's what you want. Just ask the guy who runs this motel. He can give you directions. Darla will be looking forward to meeting you, Miss Wade. So long."

Rebecca leaned back against the cheap wooden door and listened to Glen Ballard striding away. He was whistling.

Kyle was pounding arrogantly on the door before Ballard had driven out of the lot.

"Open up, Becky. I want to talk to you."

"Not now, Kyle. I've got to get ready to meet my new neighbors."

"Like hell you do. Ballard's just trying to con you. If you're smart, you won't let him within a hundred feet of you in the future."

"I'll keep your advice in mind," she called back through the door. "Now go away, Kyle."

There was silence on the other side of the door. Rebecca waited for Kyle to try another tactic, but the next sound she heard was the sophisticated growl of the Porsche's engine.

For some reason she was vaguely disappointed that Kyle had given up so quickly this time.

With a sigh she unpacked her groceries, made a sandwich and then went back to Alice Cork's journal.

Alice, she discovered after a few pages, had some illuminating observations to make on the two members of the third generation of Ballards and Stockbridges. Apparently Alice, too, had finally come to the conclusion that Glen and Kyle were not exact copies of their fathers.

A few hours later Rebecca finally located the Ballards' sprawling home in the hills outside of town. She parked her compact behind an assortment of vehicles that ranged from a new Mercedes to a fifteen-year-old pick-up truck. It look as if most of the local community had been invited to tonight's barbecue.

She walked up the stone path to the back of the house where a sizable crowd of laughing, chatting people was clustered around a large pool. A number of children flitted around, shouting and giggling. The fragrance of wood smoke and broiling meat filled the air. As Rebecca hesitated, wondering which of the women present was her hostess, one of them came toward her with a wide smile of welcome.

"You must be Rebecca Wade. I'm Darla Ballard. And I'm so glad you could make it. I told Glen it would be a miracle if you showed up. I'm sure you've had all you want of Stockbridges and Ballards."

"I couldn't resist the offer of a meal somewhere besides the café in town. I've had my hamburger quota for the month," Rebecca said. She assessed Darla quickly. Glen Ballard's wife was a lovely brown-eyed blonde. She was about Rebecca's age, and she was obviously pregnant. The condition seemed to suit her. Darla was glowing.

"A free meal is the least we can offer. Come with me. I want you to meet everyone. Heaven knows they've all heard about you by now. Nothing happens between Stockbridges and Ballards around here that stays private. I understand you amazed and astounded the entire clientele of Cully's this afternoon. They're calling you the new town marshal, you know. Word has it you actually walked into the local saloon all by yourself and kept the peace, just like in the bad old days when the guys in black hats tried to shoot it out."

"It wasn't quite that colorful." Rebecca followed her hostess into the crowd thinking about how fast gossip traveled. She wondered how much malicious talk there had been when Darla had broken off her engagement to Kyle. The thought made her wince inwardly. Kyle's fierce pride must have been lacerated when his ex-fiancée had turned around and married a Ballard.

But Darla did not look like the kind of woman who would have done such a thing lightly. Rebecca tried to size her up as Darla led her through a whirl of introductions. It was obvious Darla was well liked and her smile was genuine. Rebecca realized that, with very little effort, she could like Darla, too.

"Hey, glad to see you found the place," Glen called from the smoking barbecue pits. "Give the woman a drink, honey. She probably needs one. She's been dealing with Stockbridge all day."

Darla laughed. "What would you like, Rebecca?"

"A glass of wine would be nice. You have a beautiful home here, Darla."

"Thank you. I just wish we could spend more time here," Darla said as she guided Rebecca over to where a young man in a white coat was pouring drinks. "Unfortunately Glen's business keeps us in Denver a lot of the time. Can't let the competition get ahead of Clear Advantage Development, you know."

"I'm surprised we haven't run into each other," Rebecca observed as she accepted her glass of wine.

"Are you kidding?" Darla affected wide-eyed astonishment. "Ballards and Stockbridges socialize together? Unheard of." She wrinkled her nose in a wry grimace. "Unsafe, too. No intelligent, thinking person would deliberately put a Stockbridge and a Ballard into the same room together if there was any option."

"That bad?"

"It's incredibly bad. The feud between the Ballards and the Stockbridges is legendary around these parts."

"All because of Harmony Valley?"

Darla slanted her a quick, searching glance. "It started because of the valley, but over the years a lot of other incidents have fed the fire. It's crazy, but the feud's been going on for so long now that no one has any idea of how to halt it. Sometimes I don't think any of these nice people really want to see it halted. It provides too much gossip and entertainment."

"You don't find it very entertaining, do you, Darla?" Rebecca asked softly.

Darla closed her eyes briefly. "No. I find it stupid and dangerous. But maybe that's because I've had the experience of being caught in the cross fire." She opened her eyes and gave Rebecca a level look. "I suppose you've heard all about that?"

Rebecca smiled gently. "Just the bare facts."

"Well, the bare facts are true. I was engaged to Kyle Stockbridge. And to be honest, I wouldn't be at all surprised if the primary reason Glen started courting me was precisely that I was wearing Kyle's ring. The temptation to try to take another shot at a Stockbridge was probably too much for Glen to resist, although he denies to this day that that's the sole reason he went after me. These are not nice families we're talking about, Rebecca. Believe me, I know. I was born and raised in these parts."

Rebecca chewed thoughtfully on her lower lip. "Things seemed to have worked out for you and Glen," she observed.

Darla chuckled. "They worked out because Glen got caught in his own trap. He fell in love with me. I suspect he was as surprised as I was when he realized what had happened. Kyle will always believe Glen seduced me away, but the truth is, I was on the verge of breaking off my engagement to Kyle anyway. I would have done it weeks earlier, if I'd had the nerve."

"The nerve?" Rebecca frowned.

Darla nodded and sipped at the glass of fruit juice she was holding. "It takes nerve to go up against Kyle Stockbridge. I'm sure you must have realized that by now. I had spent a lot of time agonizing over how to tell Kyle I wanted to end things when Glen showed up and made it easy. He took great pleasure in telling Kyle for me. I should never have agreed to let him do it. It was a terrible scene." She shuddered. "I'll never forget it."

Rebecca studied the throng of guests. "Why did you want to break off your engagement to Kyle?" she asked quietly.

"Two reasons," Darla said bluntly. "The first is that he was quite capable of scaring the living daylights out of me. Growing up around here, I'd heard about the Stockbridge temper, naturally, but I'd never actually faced it myself until I became engaged to Kyle."

Rebecca's eyes widened in surprise. "He frightened you?"

"I'm afraid so. Surely you've been around him long enough to see him lose his temper?"

"Well, I've certainly seen him get annoyed and heaven knows he can make a fuss when he doesn't get what he wants, but he's never really lost his temper with me."

"You're lucky. He did around me a time or two and I couldn't stand it, Rebecca," Darla explained. "It left me shaking each time. I just couldn't take it. Glen never raises his voice to me. Oh, I know he's got a temper that's the match of any Stockbridge, but he rarely displays it in front of me. Even when he does, it doesn't frighten me. Not the way Kyle frightened me."

"Kyle's temper isn't that bad." Rebecca wondered why she felt obliged to defend him. "He never really loses his self-control. But somewhere along the line he learned how to use the threat of his temper to control certain situations and he's not above exploiting that."

Darla eyed her dubiously. "He's never blown up at you?"

"I've seen him get angry at his staff, and he's yelled at me a time or two, but I've certainly never thought of him as terrifying."

"Amazing," Darla said dryly. "Whenever he got angry around me my first instinct was to run and hide. But even if I'd gotten over being nervous about that aspect of his personality, I knew I couldn't handle the other thing."

"What other thing?"

Darla slanted her another searching glance. "I didn't know how to manage the dark side of him. There was a part of him I sensed I'd never reach. We never really talked. We never communicated. Half the time I don't think he was even aware of me. He was too busy making big plans for Flaming Luck Enterprises."

"Flaming Luck certainly consumes a big portion of his life."

"It consumed all of it during the period of our engagement. Once he'd put a ring on my finger, it was as if he'd completed one more business deal. He was ready to turn his attention to another one. I felt left out. I realized he didn't really need me. He didn't love me. I came to the conclusion he might not be capable of loving anyone. That's when I knew I had to end the engagement."

"Did you love him?" It was a hard question to ask but Rebecca had to know.

Darla tilted her head to one side, considering the matter. "I'm not sure. Whatever I felt didn't last too long, so it probably wasn't real love, although it might have grown into the real thing if I'd ever gotten any response from him. I do know I was very excited and thrilled when Kyle first started dating me. He was, after all, the son of one of the most important families in the area. And at first I think the darkness in him actually attracted me. It was a challenge, I suppose."

"Kyle can certainly be a challenge," Rebecca admitted.

"Well, I got tired of the challenge when I realized I didn't have the power to change him. I knew I needed a man who was more easygoing most of the time. More open." Darla grinned. "The only time Glen gets difficult is when he's confronting Kyle. On those occasions the atmosphere takes on all the nuances of high noon in Dodge City."

"I can't believe those two have been at each other's throats all these years."

"I can't, either, but it's a fact." Darla patted her rounded stomach ruefully. "I'm probably about to start another generation of battling Ballards."

"Maybe you'll get lucky and have a little girl."

Darla grinned. "That would certainly throw a monkey wrench into the works, wouldn't it? But Ballards always seem to have male children. So do Stockbridges. If Kyle marries, I'm sure there will be another macho Stockbridge coming along who will grow up thinking the lowest form of life on earth is a Ballard."

Rebecca's brows rose. She smiled at her hostess. "Don't look at me like that. It makes me nervous."

"Sorry. But I did hear that you and Kyle had been living together, and I couldn't help but wonder…?"

"We only lived together for ten days. It's over," Rebecca said flatly. "It ended when I found out just why Kyle had 'accidentally' met me in the first place."

"Harmony Valley? You just found out about it recently?"

Rebecca nodded. "The lawyers got in touch with me yesterday. I walked out on Kyle a few hours later."

"And he followed you," Darla murmured speculatively.

"Sure. He hasn't got his hands on Harmony Valley yet."

Darla's eyes narrowed. "It doesn't sound like him."

"What doesn't sound like him?"

"I don't see Kyle actually persuading a woman to move in with him just so he could get his hands on her land. He and Glen would both go a long way out of their way to get hold of Harmony Valley, but I don't think either one of them would go that far."

"Their fathers and grandfathers apparently were willing to marry for it."

"Different times, different men," Darla said philosophically. "I might be wrong about Kyle. I'll admit I never really got to know him. But I do know Glen would not have married just to get his hands on Harmony Valley." She broke off abruptly as if a thought had just struck her. "But..."

"But what?" Rebecca demanded.

Darla smiled humorously. "It occurs to me that if Kyle had stumbled into a situation that provided the best of both worlds, he wouldn't have hesitated to make the most of it. Glen might have done the same before he met me. There's no getting around the fact that Ballards and Stockbridges take advantage of their opportunities."

"In other words, if Kyle found himself attracted to the woman who happened to own Harmony Valley, he'd take both," Rebecca concluded bluntly.

"If he could get both. The Stockbridges have always been known for their business luck," Darla said with a soft laugh. "But not their charm. Folks around here will tell you the Ballards were the first in line when the charm was being handed out. Anyway, enough of this depressing talk. Let's go see if we can find a steak with your name on it. Glen's at his best when he's standing in front of a barbecue. He says it's in the blood."

The next hour passed quickly. Rebecca began to relax and enjoy herself. Glen Ballard was busy with his other guests and made no effort to bring up the subject of Harmony Valley. Darla introduced Rebecca to several more of her friends, and the conversation turned easily on a variety of noncontroversial subjects. It was obvious everyone was far too polite to bring up the matter of the Stockbridge-Ballard feud or Rebecca's role in it.

Rebecca was beginning to wonder if she might like to keep Harmony Valley. She could have a new house built on it, she thought, a place she could use on the weekends. She smiled grimly, wondering how Kyle and Glen would react if they found out yet another independent female had chosen Harmony Valley for her home.

Rebecca was in the middle of a conversation with a rancher's wife when she first became aware of the disturbance near the swimming pool. It wasn't much in the beginning, just a murmur of awareness that hummed through the crowd. But a moment later she heard her new acquaintance gasp.

"Oh, my Lord, it's Kyle Stockbridge," the woman said. "He's here. Over by the pool. Will you look at that? Talk about nerve. Poor Darla." Scandalized horror and excitement were mirrored in her face. "I hope there won't be a scene." Her tone implied that there would very probably be a scene—that she and everyone else would be extremely disappointed if there wasn't a scene.

Rebecca turned around and saw Kyle standing near the pool. He hadn't bothered to change his clothes. He was still wearing the snug jeans, scuffed boots and faded denim shirt he'd had on earlier in the day. His black hat was jammed down over his eyes and his expression was full of sardonic challenge. He was here to make trouble and he didn't care who knew it. He caught Rebecca's eye and smiled coldly.

Before Rebecca could move, she saw Glen Ballard start through the crowd, a can of beer in each hand. She breathed a sigh of relief. Glen, at least, apparently was going to try to avoid a scene. Rebecca lost sight of the two men as the crowd shifted position.

"I should have known Kyle would pull a stunt like this. It's just like him to crash the party. He won't want you left in our clutches for very long."

Rebecca glanced at Darla who had appeared to stand beside her. She looked unhappily resigned to disaster. "It looks like Glen is going to be civil. Kyle won't make a scene if Glen refuses to respond to it."

There was a muffled snort from the rancher's wife. "Those two will make a scene anywhere, anytime."

"I'm afraid she's right," Darla said. "Neither of them can resist baiting the other. My party is going to be ruined. I just know it."

"How much of a disaster can they cause?" Rebecca asked, exasperated. "They're a couple of respectable businessmen, not two gunslingers. They aren't likely to start brawling at a party, for heaven's sake."

The rancher's wife and Darla both stared at her with pitying looks.

Rebecca blinked. "You mean they might actually start a fight? Right here in front of everyone?"

"It's happened before," the rancher's wife announced.

"When?" Rebecca was truly astounded. This was a civilized party, not a tavern.

"The most notable occasion was my wedding reception," Darla said grimly. "But there have been other instances."

"I don't believe it. Two intelligent, full-grown men?"

"Wait and see," the rancher's wife intoned knowingly.

Rebecca swung around and started through the crowd. "No, I don't think I'll wait and see. I'm going to put a stop to this right now. Kyle has no business ruining your party, Darla."

"Rebecca, wait," Darla said urgently. "Come back here. Believe me, you don't want to get in the middle of whatever is going on. There's nothing anyone can do. I heard how you handled things this afternoon, but you mustn't count on being able to do it a second time. You probably just took them both by surprise. You aren't likely to get lucky again. Trust me, this is a serious feud. It's for real. Ballards and Stockbridges always quarrel when they run into each other."

Rebecca ignored her. The crowd parted with suspicious eagerness as she made her way swiftly to poolside. When the last of the guests stepped out of her way, she found herself within a couple of feet of the two men. She was stunned to hear a familiar topic of conversation.

"I'll give you credit, Ballard," Kyle was saying. "You nearly pulled it off. But I recognized your hand behind the scenes as soon as my man started trying to explain why Jamison had changed his mind. I know your style. You'll be happy to know I got Jamison's name on that contract Monday afternoon."

Glen shrugged. "It was worth a shot," he said, taking a swallow of his beer. "When I found out you'd gotten to Jamison first on the bank deal, I was a might perturbed."

"You're getting slow in your old age, Ballard," Kyle taunted.

"I'm only six months older than you, Stockbridge, and I can still whip you with one hand tied behind my back."

"You never could take me and you know it. Remember what happened at the wedding? You wound up face-down in the punch."

"And you wound up with a face full of wedding cake, as I recall. Hope your style has improved. Not much fun beating up a guy who trips over his own feet. Like shooting fish in a barrel."

"Shooting fish in a barrel is about your speed," Kyle said derisively. "You can't handle anything tougher than that."

"I can handle you any day of the week and you know it. But I'd just as soon not have to do it here. Darla doesn't approve of public brawling." He caught sight of Rebecca. "And I get the feeling Becky doesn't approve of it, either—do you, Becky?" He gave her a wide grin.

"No, I do not." Rebecca glared at Kyle. "What are you doing here?"

"My invitation got lost in the mail but I knew Ballard would be disappointed if I didn't show."

She heard the slight slur in his voice and was genuinely shocked. "Are you drunk, Kyle?"

"Not too drunk to rip off Ballard's arm and beat him to a pulp with it." Kyle braced his feet slightly apart in a fighter's stance and took a long

swallow of beer. He kept his eyes on his opponent. "Well, Ballard? You gonna try to throw me
out of your party?"

"If I decide to throw you out, there won't be
any 'try' about it. I'll do it. Period."

"Just like you *tried* to snaffle Jamison away
from Flaming Luck?" Kyle scoffed.

"Stop it, Kyle," Rebecca hissed, furious with
him. "You're causing a scene. I won't have it."

Kyle and Glen both looked at her as if she were
incredibly naive.

"So what?" Kyle asked pointedly. "I've had
some time to think about it, and I've decided you
won't sell Harmony Valley to a bunch of weirdos.
Your threat has lost its teeth, lady. I don't buy it
any longer."

"This is a very nice party and you're going to
ruin it if you don't behave in a civilized manner,"
Rebecca snapped.

"Yeah," Glen drawled. "You're going to ruin
things, Stockbridge. You're going to cause a nasty
little scene. Shock the neighbors. Maybe you'd
better leave before you have to be carried out."

"There's only one way I'll leave here, Ballard,
and that's with Becky. I came here to get her and
I'm not going home without her."

Rebecca glared at Kyle. "I'll leave when I'm
good and ready. I'm a guest here, and I intend to
enjoy myself. I was having a lovely evening until
you arrived."

"The hell you were."

Glen Ballard grinned again. "I'm real happy to

hear you've been enjoying yourself, Miss Wade. Darla has certainly taken to you. Says the two of you are going to be good friends. That's nice, seeing as how we're going to be neighbors."

"Don't listen to him, Becky," Kyle said through his teeth. "You don't want to have anything to do with this jerk."

"Why not?" she demanded furiously.

"Because he's a Ballard," Kyle roared. "And you belong to me, remember?" Heads turned quickly. The whole crowd was listening to the confrontation taking place beside the swimming pool.

Rebecca shivered. She had told Darla earlier that Kyle had never really frightened her, but she had to admit that there were times when he certainly made her aware of his displeasure. "Keep your voice down, Kyle. You're embarrassing me."

"And you're embarrassing Darla, too, Stockbridge. Why don't you just leave?" Glen's taunting smile gleamed in the lamplight. "And don't you worry about Rebecca. We'll take real good care of her."

"You're not going to get your hooks into her," Kyle shot back. He tossed his beer can aside and stood with his hands on his hips.

"Kyle, stop it this minute. Do you hear me?" Rebecca gritted, growing alarmed. The brushfire these two men had created was escalating rapidly out of control. "You've had too much to drink and you're acting like an idiot."

"I'll go along with that," Glen Ballard said

cheerfully. "You're acting like an idiot, Stock-bridge. But, then, I guess it runs in the blood, doesn't it?"

"You want me to leave, Ballard? Why don't you try throwing me out?" Kyle unbuttoned the cuff of one shirt and started rolling up the sleeve.

"Don't mind if I do," Glen said, setting down his beer can.

"Kyle! Don't you dare start a fight here. Do you hear me?" Rebecca raged. "Don't you dare."

"Stay out of this, Becky." He didn't look at her. His attention was on his opponent.

"I will not stay out of this," she hissed. "Stop it right now, or so help me…"

But Kyle was paying absolutely no attention. He was readying himself for the fight. Glen Ballard had rolled up his own sleeves and dropped into a fighter's crouch.

"I don't believe this," Rebecca stared at first one man and then the other. "I just don't believe it. I'm going to put a stop to this right here and now."

She planted both hands on Kyle's shoulders and shoved with all of her might. With a yelp of outrage, he toppled into the pool.

"Now why didn't I think of that?" Darla Ballard said, moving up behind her husband who was doubling over in laughter at the sight of his opponent sinking under water.

Darla pushed hard and a second later Glen Ballard joined his nemesis in the swimming pool.

EIGHT

The crowd that was gathered around the pool held its collective breath as the two would-be combatants surfaced. Without a word both men stroked to the edge of the pool. The laughter didn't start until each hauled himself up over the edge and got to his feet.

Kyle and Glen stood there dripping wet and contemplating Rebecca and Darla with expressions of disgusted amazement.

"I think I'd better take this one home," Rebecca said, stepping forward to clasp Kyle by his arm. "He's in no condition to drive and if he hangs around here in those wet clothes he'll probably catch a chill. The image of a big, macho gunfighter with a bad cold doesn't do much for the imagination, does it?"

"She's right, Glen." Darla surveyed her husband. "You'd better go change your clothes, too. It's getting cool out here. Run along now."

Glen muttered something unintelligible and then meekly turned and headed for the house.

"This way, sport." Rebecca started to lead an unresisting Kyle through the amused crowd. "Good night, Darla. I enjoyed myself up until these two decided to stage their big showdown. Maybe we can get together again one of these days?"

"I'll look forward to it," Darla murmured. She saw Rebecca as far as the edge of the patio. "You know, this night will probably go down in local history."

"Why?" Rebecca asked.

"Because for the second time in one day someone tried to stop a Ballard and a Stockbridge from getting into a fight."

"We not only tried," Rebecca pointed out, "we succeeded."

"Thanks to you. Obviously Ballards and Stockbridges aren't quite as tough as they've led everyone to believe over the years," Darla remarked thoughtfully.

Kyle stiffened under Rebecca's hand but he said nothing. Rebecca smiled fleetingly.

"We didn't witness a show of weakness on either side back there, Darla," Rebecca said. "What we saw was a demonstration of common sense. Apparently, contrary to popular myth, given a big enough hint, even a Ballard or a Stockbridge can figure out when to quit. I think that's a very hopeful sign. See you later."

"I'll see you get your car tomorrow," Darla called. "How about lunch?"

"Sounds great," Rebecca called back.

Darla laughed as she waved farewell. "I think this is the part where I'm supposed to ask 'Who was that masked lady?' as you ride off into the sunset." She turned and went back toward the pool where the crowd was busy rehashing the scene that had just taken place. Rebecca had a hunch everyone in the community would be discussing the events for days.

Kyle spoke for the first time, his voice low and grumbling. "If you two get any friendlier you'll have to form a club."

"Not a bad idea. We could call it the Society of Ladies Interested in Stopping the Stockbridge-Ballard Feud."

Kyle shot her a dark glance. "What do you care about the feud? You're planning to sell to Ballard and head back for Denver."

"Am I?"

"Isn't that why you were here tonight? To hear Ballard's offer?"

"Nope. I came out of curiosity. And because I wanted to meet my new neighbors."

"Sure you did."

"It's the truth." They approached the black Porsche, which was parked at the end of the driveway. "Let me have your keys, Kyle."

He reached into the wet pocket of his jeans and fished out the keys, but he didn't turn them over to Rebecca. "I'll drive."

"No, you will not drive. You've had too much to drink."

Kyle hesitated, shrugged and handed over his

keys. "Take it easy," was all he said. He climbed
into the passenger seat, heedless of the damage
his wet clothes might do to the upholstery. "Turn
right on the road at the end of the driveway. You
ever been behind the wheel of a Porsche before?"
He fastened his seat belt.

"No, but a car's a car, isn't it?" Rebecca blithely
shoved the key into the ignition and fumbled
with the gears. "I've been driving for years."

Kyle winced but stoically said nothing as finely
meshed machinery ground in protest. Rebecca
got the car in motion and spun the wheel. The
Porsche jerked violently to the right.

"Tight steering," she remarked as she straightened out the nose of the Porsche and headed for
the road at the bottom of the driveway.

"Very." Kyle's voice was even tighter than the
steering.

Rebecca slid her passenger a sidelong glance
and stifled a small grin.

Her amusement faded, however, as she sped
down the road. She lapsed into a silence that was
thicker than Kyle's. It wasn't until she had driven
over five miles that she began to get suspicious.

"You're taking this whole thing amazingly
well," Rebecca finally observed.

Kyle leaned his head back against the seat and
closed his eyes. "Win some—lose some," he
stated with admirable sangfroid.

The truth dawned on Rebecca slowly. "I get it,"
she said finally. "You think you won tonight,
don't you? You succeeded in accomplishing what

you set out to do. You crashed the Ballard's party and got me out of their clutches. Congratulations.''

Kyle didn't open his eyes. "Thanks. The victory wasn't without its down side. I didn't count on ending up in the pool.''

"I suppose you weren't even as drunk as you appeared?'' Rebecca's hands tightened on the wheel.

"The only thing I had to drink was half of that can of beer Ballard gave me.''

"I see.''

Kyle opened his eyes then, his gaze shadowed in the dark confines of the car. "No, you don't, but maybe you will one of these days. Take a left up here where that other road joins this one.''

Rebecca obeyed, wondering if she should be furious at the deception. She couldn't seem to work up the energy. Too many other things were going through her mind.

"You can't afford to hang around here keeping an eye on me for long, Kyle. You've got a company to run back in Denver.''

"I'm practicing delegating authority, just like you taught me. I left Harrison in charge.''

"You left Rick in charge?'' Rebecca was amazed. "After the way you chewed him out for nearly losing the Jamison deal?''

"He's got a lot to learn,'' Kyle muttered, "but he's basically smart enough to hold things together for a few days. You told me that, yourself, once. Remember?''

"I didn't think you were listening."

"I always listen to you, Becky. You ought to know that by now."

Rebecca was silent for a while, turning that over in her mind. "I read an interesting passage in Alice Cork's journal today," she said finally.

"Yeah?" Kyle didn't sound encouraging.

"It was about something that happened on a Halloween night several years ago. Back when you and Glen Ballard were teenagers. Alice wrote that she had some trouble that night."

"Kids get up to all kinds of things on Halloween."

"She noted that a gang of boys from the neighboring town decided to trash her barn as a Halloween prank."

"The kids used to tell each other she was a witch."

"She was worried about her livestock that night. Afraid some of the animals might be injured," Rebecca continued.

"Alice always did like animals."

"She wrote in her journal that she was nervous. She wasn't sure what to do. There were a number of boys involved, some of them quite rough. She figured she couldn't just start shooting. They were, after all, just kids."

"I didn't realize old Alice had such fine scruples. God knows she was always willing enough to wave her shotgun in my face."

Rebecca ignored that. "Alice was scared that

night, Kyle. Scared for her animals and maybe a little scared for herself, too."

"I didn't think anything could scare Alice Cork."

"She was a woman living alone in an isolated area. Of course, she got nervous at times. Anyone would."

"You never even met the woman," Kyle muttered. "How do you know what she felt?"

"I just know. At any rate, she wrote that, in the end, she didn't have to worry after all. A couple of teenage boys, local kids, drove up in a pickup truck that belonged to the Stockbridge ranch. The two boys got out of the truck and proceeded to beat the stuffing out of a couple of the bigger kids who were trying to trash the barn. The rest of the gang ran off into the night. The two boys who had saved Alice's barn and maybe her animals got back in the truck and drove away."

"Who would have thought old Alice would have kept such a detailed journal?"

"That was you driving the pickup that night, wasn't it, Kyle? You're the one who ran off that gang of toughs who were threatening Alice."

"I had help."

"I know. Glen Ballard."

There was silence from the other side of the Porsche. "Alice saw us both?"

"Oh, yes. She saw you and Glen. She knew who had come to her rescue. She wrote in her diary that there might be hope for the next generation of Ballards and Stockbridges, after all. When the chips were down, apparently, the two of you could put aside the feud long enough to work together."

"Don't forget that Ballard and I both had a long-term interest in Harmony Valley," Kyle said. "You may have noticed we're both kind of possessive about it. Neither of us was about to let a bunch of young toughs trash Alice's barn that night. We took it personally, I guess you could say. When I heard about the plans for Halloween, I borrowed Dad's truck and went to find Ballard. I knew I was going to need a little help. I figured he had a vested interest in the situation, same as I did."

"Where did you find Glen that night?"

"He was cruising town with a bunch of his friends. I told him what was happening and he got in the truck without asking any questions. We drove over to Harmony Valley and took care of the problem. Then I drove Ballard back to town and dropped him off in front of the gas station. End of story. We never said more than ten words to each other during the whole thing."

Rebecca nodded thoughtfully. "But Alice knew what had happened."

Kyle shrugged again. "And based on that one incident, she came to the conclusion Ballard and I could some day coexist?"

"I think Alice Cork was a very perceptive woman. And there have been other incidents, haven't there, Kyle? Not very many, I'll grant you, but one or two. Alice wrote about how you and Glen split the cost of Herb Crocket's bypass surgery a few years ago. The Crockets didn't have any insurance at the time."

Kyle swore bluntly. "She knew about that, too? No one was supposed to know about that. I told Ethel to send the hospital bill to me and keep quiet about it. But Ballard got wind of what was happening and demanded to split the tab with me."

"And you let him."

"Hell, yes. I let him. You got any idea what by-pass surgery costs? At the time I wasn't nearly as well off as I am today. Neither was Ballard. It made sense for both of us to go fifty-fifty instead of one of us trying to cover the whole thing. Besides, we'd both known Herb all our lives."

"Just common sense, hmm? Naturally you'd both want to make certain no one found out you and Glen were capable of cooperating. Bad for the image."

"Believe me. It wasn't what you'd call real co-operation, Becky. Don't romanticize it. And don't get any ideas about riding into town on a noble white steed and ending the Stockbridge-Ballard feud, either. Life doesn't work that way. Turn right here."

Rebecca swung the wheel a bit sharply and Kyle grabbed at the dashboard. "Sorry," she said lightly.

"I can tell." He threw her a dangerous glance. "The house is at the end of this driveway. Up there on that hill."

Rebecca peered ahead. Lights were on inside the sprawling, two-story ranch home, but the illumination didn't seem to project a feeling of warmth. In the dark it was hard to see much, but she got an impression of a house built for grim endurance. There were other large structures out back that looked like stables.

"You can park over there," Kyle said, indicating a stretch of concrete in front of a large garage.

Rebecca obeyed and switched off the engine. "You must be freezing in those wet clothes."

"The thrill of your driving kept me warm." Kyle pushed open his door. "But now that you bring up the subject, I realize you're right. I'm freezing. I need a hot shower and a glass of brandy. Let's get into the house before I also need treatment for hypothermia."

He held out his hands for his keys as they hurried up the front steps. Rebecca hesitated and then handed them over to him. Later she would figure out how she was going to get back to the motel.

"You pour the brandy," Kyle said as he opened the front door and ushered her into the living room. "It's over there by the fireplace. I'm going to get out of these clothes." He yanked at the buttons of his wet shirt. "Be back in a few minutes."

Rebecca watched him stride down the hall, peeling off his shirt as he went. He certainly didn't seem nearly as upset about the dunking as she would have expected. But, then, that was probably because Kyle figured he'd won the confrontation with Glen Ballard. He'd gotten what he wanted. Rebecca had gone home with him.

Shaking her head ruefully, Rebecca crossed the room to the mahogany table beside the fireplace. The brandy glasses were fashioned of beautifully cut crystal, she noted. They looked old. And the brandy was about as old as the crystal, according to the label.

The glasses were the only touch of elegance or luxury in the room. She wondered if they had been wedding gifts that Martha Stockbridge had left behind when she had fled.

Everything else in the place looked heavy, masculine, functional and cold. It was a man's room, with no touch of softness or charm to lighten the oppressive atmosphere. Rebecca tried to imagine what effect a house like this would have had on a young, motherless boy. There had been no softness in Kyle's life, Alice Cork had written. Kyle had been raised by a hard, bitter, withdrawn man, a man who would have scorned a woman's touch.

Kyle returned less than fifteen minutes later, buttoning a fresh shirt as he came down the hall. There was an exuberance in his stride that told its own story. It was clear he had the rest of the evening planned.

"The Stockbridge luck seems to be running true to form again, I take it?" Rebecca asked speculatively as she handed him a glass of brandy.

"Stockbridge luck beats Ballard charm any day of the week." He took a swallow of the brandy.

"Except when it comes to women," she reminded him smoothly. He eyed her over the rim of the glass. "Did you love her very much, Kyle?"

He looked blank. "Who?"

Rebecca frowned. "Darla."

"Oh, Darla." He made a dismissing gesture with one hand. "I told you about her. It's ancient history."

"So is the Stockbridge-Ballard feud, but it still persists."

Kyle's gaze grew sharp and speculative. "Are you jealous, Becky?" he asked suddenly.

"I'm curious, that's all." She turned away and walked over to stand in front of the cold fireplace.

"You *are* jealous." Kyle spoke with satisfaction as he set down his brandy glass and went down on one knee to build a fire.

"No, damn it. I am not jealous!"

"Forget Darla," Kyle broke in crisply as he adjusted kindling. "I'm not carrying the torch. I'll admit I was a tad upset when she picked Ballard to run off with, but I'm over it." He grinned and waved a long fireplace match aloft. "You're the only one who lights a fire under me, baby."

"You asked her to marry you."

"That was four long years ago." He glanced up and saw the assessing look in her eyes. "Hey," Kyle said softly as he finished lighting the fire and got to his feet. "What's the problem here?"

"I told you. I'm curious. That's all."

He caught her shoulders, the indulgent humor

fading from his face. "I've told you about Darla. She's not important any longer."

"She says you might not have even noticed the engagement had ended if it hadn't been for the fact that Ballard was waiting in the wings. A Stockbridge can't stand to lose anything to a Ballard."

"True enough," he said with a sigh. "But I got even. I'm satisfied on that score."

"Did you really make a scene at their wedding?" After all she had learned about this man, that sort of audacity was still enough to amaze her.

Kyle shook his head reminiscingly and ignored the question. "You know, right up until the last minute, I thought for sure Ballard was just using Darla to get at me. I never expected him to marry her. But I guess things have been for real between them after all. They seem happy together."

"They are. And if it's any consolation, Darla was afraid she was being used, too. But she loved Glen and decided to take a chance. She says he got caught in his own trap. He fell in love with her in spite of himself."

Kyle slid his hands into his back pockets and stared down into the fire. "Ballard's not the only one who got caught in a trap. I got caught in one, too. I want you back, Becky."

She held her breath. "Why? So you can be assured of getting Harmony Valley?"

"No, damn it, not because of Harmony Valley! You've got a one-track brain, woman."

"You're the one who put my brain on that particular track."

Kyle groaned. "I know. I know. I made a mess of things. I admit it." He turned and gave her a direct look. His eyes were intense and brilliant in the firelight. "But I'll do whatever it takes to get you back."

"Whatever it takes?" she repeated uncertainly.

He paused and then said grimly, "I suppose you want me to prove how serious I am about getting you back. I've done a lot of thinking, Becky. And I'm prepared to do exactly that."

Rebecca was suddenly very uneasy with the direction of the conversation. Kyle Stockbridge was a wily opponent. He knew all the tricks and he was not above using the vast majority of them. "It's not a question of proving anything," she said carefully.

"I think it is," he countered quietly. "I think that things are so tangled up now that you'll never believe how important you are to me unless I show you."

She didn't look at him. "How can you do that?"

"What would you say," he asked slowly, "if I told you to go ahead and sell Harmony Valley to Ballard?"

Rebecca's head snapped around. "Sell to Ballard?"

He nodded, saying nothing else.

"You'd hit the roof if I did that. You'd explode. You'd be furious. You'd never forgive me, let alone want me back."

Kyle shook his head, still saying nothing. But he watched her unblinkingly.

Rebecca toyed with her brandy glass. "I don't understand."

"I'm trying to prove something to you, Becky. I don't know any other way to do it."

"But, Kyle..."

He took a step forward and gently removed the glass from her hand. "I want you more than I want that damned land." He caught her face between his palms. "And I want you to know it."

Kyle bent his head and took her mouth with a slow, seductive heat that left Rebecca trembling. She touched his wrists, his arms and then, with a small sigh of surrender, she clung to him.

"That's it, baby," he breathed, folding her close. "That's it. Stop fighting me. Come back to me. Let me show you how much I want you."

The hurt and anger that had driven Rebecca away from him melted in the warmth of Kyle's embrace. This was where she wanted to be, she thought. She loved him. Nothing could change that, just as nothing on earth could alter the thrilling sensation she experienced when Kyle made love to her.

"I have a feeling I'm going to regret this."

"No you won't. I'll make sure you don't. It's okay, Becky," Kyle murmured reassuringly against her throat. "Everything's going to be okay between us again. You'll see. Give me a chance to show you." The soothing, gentling words were punctuated by a series of hungry kisses.

"I wish I understood," Rebecca whispered helplessly.

"There's nothing to understand except the way I feel about you. This is where you belong, Becky. Right here in my arms."

Abandoning herself to instinct, Rebecca allowed herself to be drawn into his heat. He was right. This was where she belonged. She pressed against him, aware of his response in every fiber of her being. Kyle made no secret out of the fact that his physical reaction to her was fierce and immediate.

And she knew there was little she could do to hide her own response. On this level, they were equal.

Rebecca felt Kyle's fingers on the fastening of her blouse. He removed the garment with a restrained eagerness that was oddly touching. He was trying to control himself, she realized, trying not to rush her.

She raised her face and kissed the hard line of his jaw. "It's all right," she heard herself whisper and knew he understood when he groaned and hugged her close.

"I want to do it right. I want to show you," Kyle said huskily as he unpinned her hair. He caught the dark brown mass in his fingers.

Rebecca smiled tremulously. "You always do it right. It's never been anything but right with you." And that was the truth, she thought.

"Oh, Becky," he rasped. "My sweet, soft, sexy Becky. You make me crazy."

He undressed her quickly, his hands moving over her fire-warmed skin. When the last of her clothing lay in a small heap at her feet, Kyle grazed his thumb over one breast. When the nipple grew taut, he smiled with satisfaction and leaned down to kiss it.

"Kyle." His name was a throaty catch of her breath. Rebecca closed her eyes and slid her hands inside his shirt. The tight, muscled strength of him was as alluring as ever.

He let her push his shirt off and moved her fingers lower. He hadn't bothered to fasten the metal snap on his jeans. When she began to fumble with the zipper he caught her fingers. "You're trembling." He seemed pleased with this small show of the depths of her response.

"I know. I can't help it."

"I'm glad. Do you know what it does to me?"

"What?"

"Find out for yourself, although you ought to know by now." He guided her fingers back to his zipper and helped her ease it down. Then he pushed her hand inside his briefs. "Oh, baby," he muttered as she cupped him intimately. *"Baby."*

He was hot and heavy and aroused. He filled her fingers, straining against her. When Rebecca stroked him lightly, he groaned in response and pushed his hips against her, urging her to caress him more firmly.

Then he impatiently kicked away the jeans and briefs. In the firelight he looked very primitve and very male.

His hands slid warmly down her back to her buttocks. He squeezed slowly, fingers flexing in the soft flesh until she was shivering.

When she sighed his name against his chest, Kyle eased her down onto the rug in front of the fire. She opened her eyes to find him leaning over her, gazing down at her with a glittering passion that took away her breath.

"Kyle?"

"Did you really think you could just walk away from me?" He trapped one of her legs beneath his heavy thigh and kissed her thoroughly. His tongue penetrated deep for a long moment, reasserting his claim to her warmth. "Did you think I'd let you go after what we've found together?"

Rebecca had no answer for that. She wrapped her arms around him, accepting the force of the physical attraction that existed between them and accepting, too, the power of her own love.

Kyle responded instantly to the silent, feminine summons. He parted her thighs and lowered himself between them.

"Wrap yourself around me," he urged thickly. "Hold me tight, baby."

She obeyed, aware of his throbbing maleness at the entrance to her softness. When she twisted her legs around his waist, he muttered encouragement and began to push himself into her.

Rebecca moaned softly as Kyle filled her. She tightened around him, pulling him deeper into her body. Then he began to move with slow, deliberate strokes that inflamed her senses. He knew her so well already, she realized. He knew exactly how to send her into the heart of the whirlwind.

Within seconds she ached for him. Within minutes she couldn't get enough of him. Her nails sank into his back, her hips lifted demandingly and her cries were soft, imperious commands that seemed to inflame Kyle.

"Touch me," she begged.

"How?"

"You know how," she said quickly. "The way you always do."

"I've forgotten."

"Kyle!"

"Show me how you want it."

"Please, Kyle. Now. Touch me *now*."

"I'll do whatever you want, baby. You know that. All you have to do is show me how you want it." He gave her his hand.

He was teasing her, and she was in no mood for it. She was on fire. She caught his fingers and guided them awkwardly down between their bodies. "There," she said breathlessly. "Touch me there. The way you always do."

"Like this?" His fingers danced across her intimately, and Rebecca thought she would fly apart.

"*Yes.*" She arched furiously against him. "Again."

"Such a demanding little cat." But he repeated the tantalizing movement until she was crying out his name in shuddering ecstasy.

Kyle lost his own self-control at that point.

"*Becky.*" He drove into her one last time, plunging himself to the hilt of her softness. His body arched violently and his shout of satisfaction filled the room.

For a long time there was only the flicker of firelight and the crackle of burning wood. Rebecca felt warm and safe, tucked way from reality. She nestled against Kyle's lean, strong body and refused to think of the future. Tonight all was as it should be.

Kyle's mouth curved faintly as he watched her. After a little while he got to his feet, picked her up in his arms and carried her down the hall to his bedroom.

The dawn light filtered slowly through the window. Kyle awoke and lay quietly for a moment, watching the sunrise as he had every morning in his lonely childhood. But this morning everything was different. This morning he was no longer alone.

The comfortable, sensual, delightfully familiar warmth of the woman lying next to him was having the usual effect on him. He realized he was already addicted to the pleasures of waking up beside Rebecca.

He turned on his side and trailed his hand lightly down her shoulder and over her thigh. She stirred and stretched like a sleek little seal. Then she turned her head on the pillow and looked up at him from under half-closed lashes.

"It can't be morning already," Rebecca said.

"It is. But we're in no rush."

She yawned. "Then why did you wake me?"

"Courtesy. I thought you'd like to be awake when I make love to you." He kissed her shoulder, indulging himself in the taste of her.

"Thoughtful of you, but I assure you there's very little chance I could sleep through your love-making." Her amber eyes glinted at him from beneath her long lashes.

"Why, thank you, ma'am," he drawled in his best cowboy twang. "I'll take that as a compliment. Us country boys do our best, but it's always nice to hear a sophisticated city girl like yourself say she appreciates the effort."

"Just keep up the good work and I'm sure you'll go far." She glanced around the room, taking in the dark, solid furnishings and bare walls. "Do you spend a lot of time here, Kyle?"

He followed her gaze. "Not as much as I'd like. I've been busy for the past few years."

"Yes, I know. Building your company." Rebecca sat up slowly, hugging her knees.

He frowned. "You say that as if it were a crime. A firm like Flaming Luck Enterprises doesn't get where it is without a lot of hard work."

She shook her head quickly. "I know that."

"You don't sound very approving."

"It's just that you tend to get obsessed with things, Kyle. Your company, Harmony Valley…"

"And you," he growled, reaching out to pull her back down beside him. He leaned over her. "I'm obsessed with you, Becky. I've wanted you since the first day I saw you. And I'm going to make damned sure you believe me. I meant what I said last night. Sell the valley to Ballard, if that's what it will take to make you realize you're more important to me than that hunk of land."

She lay quietly staring up at him for a long moment. "It's all right. We don't have to play this game."

He was momentarily baffled. "What game?"

She moved her head slowly on the pillow, a wry smile touching her soft mouth. "You know what I'm talking about. All that nonsense about encouraging me to sell the valley to Glen Ballard. You know me well enough to guess I'd never take you up on it. Just like you knew I'd never really sell the valley to some weird cult. I'd never ask you to prove yourself that way."

Kyle couldn't quite stifle the rush of relief that went through him, but he still didn't understand what she was saying. "Let me get this straight. You're not going to sell to Ballard after all?"

"You know I would never turn all of Harmony Valley over to him. Deep down, I'm sure you've known that all along. Isn't that why you made the grand gesture last night? Because you knew I wouldn't take you up on it?"

Kyle finally realized just what she was thinking. Righteous indignation flared within him. "You think I was faking it? You don't believe I meant it when I said to sell the land to Ballard if that would prove I wanted you?"

She touched his shoulder, her fingers gentle on

his skin. "I've worked for you for over two months, Kyle. You are one savvy poker player when it comes to business games. But I've seen you bluff before."

"I was not bluffing, damn it!" Kyle caught her wrists and pinned them above her head. He was angry now, but he controlled his temper, desperate to make her understand that his grand gesture, as she termed it, had been for real. "I meant every word I said last night. I wasn't playing games, Becky. You've got to believe that."

She shook her head ruefully. "You took a risk, you know. I was mad enough yesterday to actually consider selling the whole valley to Ballard."

"Sell it, if it will satisfy you," he grated.

"I couldn't do that. It means too much to you. I just couldn't do it," she said quietly. "And you know it. Will you let me up, please? I want to take a shower."

For an instant Kyle refused to move. He struggled furiously to think of some way to convince her his offer had been for real. His temper was near the explosive point. It was all he could do to keep from lashing out at the woman lying under him. He had to make her understand.

"Becky, listen to me. I wasn't trying to run a bluff last night. I meant what I said. Every damned word."

"Please let me up, Kyle."

He didn't want to let her up. He wanted to keep her pinned right where she was while he made love to her until she was shivering, until she couldn't possibly doubt him.

But if he used force at this juncture, she might never believe him. Frustrated, Kyle rolled over. "Go on. Take your shower. When you get out, we'll talk. I'm going to make you understand that I meant everything I said last night."

She scrambled to the side of the bed as he released her. He watched broodingly as she disappeared into the bathroom. When the door closed firmly behind her, Kyle swore again, violently.

This was one event he hadn't anticipated.

Last night he had made what had to be the noblest gesture of his entire life, and she hadn't believed a word of it. Rebecca had assumed he was bluffing.

Fury burned within him, but over and above that was a sense of desperation—a feeling that was dangerously akin to panic. *Rebecca didn't believe him.*

Kyle had dealt with a lot of problems in his life, but he had never faced the problem of rebuilding trust between himself and a woman after it had been shattered.

Rebecca's doubt seared his soul.

NINE

"It's the most fascinating thing to read," Rebecca said enthusiastically to Darla as they sat eating hamburgers in the town's one café. "A real piece of local history. Alice had a wonderful eye for details and people."

"Was she lonely out there all by herself in that valley?" Darla asked interestedly as she dipped a French fry into a pool of catsup.

Rebecca thought about what she had read in the Cork journal. "Sometimes. But no more than anyone is from time to time, I think. She really loved her farm and the animals. She seemed to take a lot of satisfaction from the day-to-day routine of that kind of life."

"Does the journal go all the way back to the time when she was engaged to marry Glen's father?"

Rebecca nodded. "That part of the record is the only truly sad portion. When she discovered that Ballard didn't love her and had seduced her in the hopes of getting Harmony Valley, Alice was crushed. When she found out she was pregnant, she was torn between a woman's rage and a mother's love. But she cried when she lost the baby. It made me cry to read that part of the journal."

"Makes you want to throttle Glen's father, doesn't it?"

"Kyle's father, too. Cale had the gall to try to seduce poor Alice, first. But he botched it. He pushed too hard and too fast, and when she resisted he lost his temper. He frightened Alice."

"And Ballard senior was waiting in the wings to charm her," Darla concluded. "Typical Ballard-Stockbridge scenario. That poor woman. She resisted the rough, dangerous one, only to fall victim to the smooth-talking seducer. And neither really cared about her. I told you the Ballards and the Stockbridges do not have a reputation for being nice folks when it comes to the subject of Harmony Valley. They've always been obsessed with that land."

"I know." Rebecca picked up her hamburger and bit into it. She was still thinking about Kyle's reaction to her this morning. She had expected him to be at least somewhat grateful that she hadn't called his bluff. Instead he had been tight-lipped with anger. When he had driven her back to the motel, she sensed he had been as close to losing his temper with her as he had ever been.

He had, in fact, acted downright insulted, now that she thought about it. Insulting dragons was probably a dangerous pastime.

"So what's the solution, Becky?" Darla asked slowly.

"Believe me, I've given it a lot of thought. I just hope I can pull it off." She shook her head. "You know, Alice wrote at the end of her journal that she had a feeling I would be able to make a difference around here. She thought I could handle Glen and Kyle and the feud. But, Darla, I never even met the woman. What made her think she should leave the property to me?"

"Who knows? She probably had one of her feelings about you. I swear the woman was downright psychic at times. Just ask anyone. If she had a feeling you were the right one to get Harmony Valley, she was probably right. I wouldn't want to be in your shoes, though. Are you going to sell the land?"

"And let Glen and Kyle harass some poor unsuspecting newcomer to the area?"

"An investor might not object to that kind of harrassment," Darla said with a chuckle. "After all, Glen and Kyle would both be offering top dollar."

"True. But it doesn't seem like the right way to handle the problem. The war would go on. This isn't a normal real-estate deal. This is personal."

"For you, or Alice Cork and her mother?" Darla asked shrewdly.

"For all three of us," Rebecca said quietly. "Three different women caught in the middle of this battle. I think it's time the opposing sides were forced to fight it out hand-to-hand."

Darla eyed her with sharp interest. "You have a plan?"

"I have a plan," Rebecca confirmed. "It came to me yesterday evening as I watched Kyle and Glen haul themselves out of your pool."

Darla grinned. "That was quite a sight, wasn't it? People will be talking about that for months. But you took a major risk when you pushed Kyle into the water. I've seen him explode on far less pretext."

Rebecca arched her brow. "I know. But as I explained, Kyle has never really lost his temper with me."

"That is astonishing, you know."

Rebecca shook her head, aware of a trace of smugness deep down inside. "I think my coworkers like me because I have a reputation for being able to walk in and out of the dragon's lair unscathed. I go where they fear to tread. And I get away with it."

"Is that right? Tell me something, Becky. After you execute this big plan of yours, do you still expect to be walking around unscathed?"

Rebecca sighed regretfully. "No. To be blunt, I expect there will be hell to pay when Kyle finds out what I'm going to do with that land."

"You don't look as if you expect your relationship to survive the aftershocks," Darla observed.

Rebecca looked at her. "I don't know what will happen," she admitted truthfully. "But I guess I'll find out for certain just how deep Kyle's feelings for me go."

"And if his feelings aren't as strong as you hope?"

"I won't be any worse off than the two other women who've had the misfortune to own Harmony Valley," Rebecca said with a calm she was far from feeling. "At least, I'll have had the satisfaction of knowing justice has been done."

The café door opened and Glen Ballard strolled in. He nodded pleasantly to the handful of people sitting around drinking coffee and then made his way to where his wife sat with Rebecca.

"Didn't you two cause enough gossip last night?" he said with a grin as he hung his gray Stetson on a nearby hook and sat down next to Darla. "You're really adding fuel to the fire by having lunch together today. Nobody can figure out what's going on."

"Keep 'em guessing is our motto," Darla said, lifting her smiling face for a quick kiss. "Rebecca was just telling me she's made a decision about what to do with Harmony Valley."

Glen's smile was still easy, but his gaze was suddenly that of a hawk sighting prey as he lounged back in the booth. "No kidding? When are you going to drop the warhead on Kyle and me?"

"Just as soon as I get the two of you together," Rebecca promised.

"Well, now, that shouldn't take too long. I saw his car over at the motel. He's looking for you right now. Won't take him long to figure out you're in here. I'd like to see the expression on his face when he recognizes my car out front."

The café door opened with a sharp crack, and this time Rebecca didn't need the murmur of interested voices to warn her who was striding into the restaurant.

Kyle came down the row of booths with his usual no-nonsense stride. He paid no attention to the waves of curiosity that filled the room.

"I've been looking for you," he said to Rebecca as he claimed the space beside her. "'Afternoon, Darla."

"Good afternoon, Kyle. I don't believe we've had a chance to chat much since my wedding. Not that we got to have much of a conversation then. You were too busy adding the special Stockbridge touch to the festivities. How are you these days?" Darla smiled with a hint of mischief.

Kyle grunted. "I'm fine. Just fine."

"Isn't it fortunate neither you nor Glen caught a chill from your dunking last night?"

Rebecca glanced at both men, who were now eyeing each other over the short distance of the Formica-topped table. "It would take more than a drenching to bring either of these two down."

Kyle ignored both women. "What are you doing here, Ballard?"

"I was about to order a burger and listen to Rebecca tell me the fate of Harmony Valley. You've got to admit I've got a vested interest."

"You have about as much legitimate interest in that land as a snake has." Kyle broke off as the waitress approached. "Bring me a cup of coffee, Jan. And a burger."

"Same for me, Jan," Glen said.

Jan nodded quickly, glanced with open curiosity at both women and then bolted for the kitchen, gum snapping loudly as usual.

"I suggest you both stop arguing over who has an interest in Harmony Valley," Rebecca said around a French fry. "Because as of now you both do."

Kyle and Glen switched glittering looks to her composed face.

"What the hell's that supposed to mean?" Kyle demanded.

"I've made my decision. I'm deeding the land over to both of you. Fifty-fifty. Joint ownership. You'll have to figure out how to share it. I know neither of you will ever sell out to the other so you're both stuck with it. I'm getting out of the picture."

Darla choked on a bite of hamburger. She gulped coffee to clear her throat, her eyes tearing. There was dead silence in the restaurant as everyone strained to overhear.

Kyle and Glen both stared at Rebecca as if she'd gone insane.

"Are you out of your mind?" Kyle finally said, his voice fierce.

"Becky, it would never work," Glen said swiftly. "Stockbridge and I couldn't manage to split an apple pie, let alone that land. We'd tear out each other's throats. It's a nice gesture, but..."

"It's not a gesture, nice or otherwise," Rebecca said bluntly. "I'm exacting a little justice here on behalf of myself, Alice Cork and her mother. Three women have suffered at the hands of Ballards and Stockbridges because of that land. Now it's your turn. You two have a choice. You can tear each other to pieces, or you can figure out how to work together to do something creative with that beautiful valley."

"There is a third alternative," Darla observed. "They could sell out to a stranger and let someone else have Harmony Valley."

"*Never*," Glen rasped.

"Not a chance in hell," Kyle confirmed instantly.

"You see?" Rebecca said to Darla. "There's hope. They can agree on some things."

"What a disaster," Glen said softly. "Leave it to a woman. She's right, Stockbridge. Alice and her mother are going to get their revenge after all."

Kyle turned on Rebecca, his face stark with the kind of rage he had never aimed at her before. "Outside," he said with a dangerous softness. "Now. I want to talk to you." He got to his feet and stood waiting for her.

Rebecca looked up into the green fury in his eyes, and a cold chill went through her. "My hamburger," she said weakly.

"Outside," he repeated in that deadly quiet tone.

Rebecca didn't say another word. She was aware of Darla watching her anxiously, but she shook her head slightly when she sensed the other woman might try to intervene.

Rebecca slid out of the booth and walked down the row of fascinated spectators without looking either to the right or the left. She kept her chin high and her back straight, aware of Kyle following hard on her heels.

Now, at last, she thought she understood just why the Stockbridge temper inspired such awe. She should have known it would end this way. She had taken a gamble and lost.

When Rebecca reached the door she opened it and stepped outside. Kyle caught her arm and hauled her over to where the Porsche was parked.

"You sneaky, conniving, manipulating little witch," he said between his teeth. "I let you get away with murder on the job at Flaming Luck but no one, *no one* gets away with trying to play games with my life the way you're trying to do. Do you hear me, Rebecca?"

"I hear you," she whispered. She looked past him, focusing on the mountains in the distance.

"Look at me when I'm talking to you, lady." He trapped her chin in his fingers and forced her to meet his furious eyes. His jaw was rigid with his anger. "That was one damned fool stunt you cooked up. You'd have your revenge, all right, if I let you go through with it. But if you think you're going to get away with it, you're crazy. I won't let any woman run me around in circles like that. *Not even you.*"

Her own temper flared. "Don't say that as if I

were ever someone special to you. We both know the truth." Her voice was tight in her throat. "The only reason you were ever interested in me was because of Harmony Valley. I'd hoped you were telling me the truth when you said your feelings for me were stronger than your obsession with that land, but I should have known better than to believe you."

"Don't you dare try to twist this around so that it comes out being a test of my feelings for you. I gave you your chance to test me. I told you to go ahead and sell to Ballard if you doubted me that much."

"You knew all along I'd never do that," Rebecca said swiftly. "It was safe for you to offer me that option because you knew I'd never take it. Maybe I should have. It would have served you right. But that way Ballard would have gotten more than he deserved, and there would have been no justice for Alice Cork."

"What right do you have to go out gunning for justice for Alice and her mother? You never even knew those two women," Kyle snarled.

"They were family."

"You'd never even heard of them before you met me."

"Then blame yourself for this whole situation. If you hadn't gone out of your way to hunt me down and seduce me, I wouldn't be handing you and Glen the problem of Harmony Valley."

"Damn it, woman, you're playing fast and

loose with my life and my future, and I won't let anyone do that."

"You can't stop me." She was amazed at the degree of courage required to stand here and confront him. Now she knew why so many quailed at the prospect of dealing with Kyle in this mood.

"Don't challenge me, Becky." There was bleak warning in his eyes. "We both know you'll lose. Don't make me your enemy. Don't do this to either of us."

"There's an option," she pointed out in a low voice.

"What option?" he snapped. "Working with Ballard? That's not an option. That's a flat-out impossibility. If you knew a little more about local history, you'd realize that. There's no way a Stockbridge can work with a Ballard. You seem to think this feud is some kind of long-standing joke. But it's not, Rebecca. Men have died in the battle between Ballard's family and mine."

"And women have cried. But that's all in the past. It's time to end it."

"You're not going to be the one to do it," he roared. "Understand me? I warned you not to try to play peacemaker. You're mine. Your loyalty is to me, not Ballard. You admitted as much this morning when you said you couldn't sell the land outright to him."

"You can't force me to choose sides. I've already made my decision and I'm sticking with it."

"Even if it tears us apart?"

She looked at him helplessly. "We were never really together, Kyle. I had a few hopes and dreams, but I see now that they were based on illusion. You've just said you think I'm a sneaky, conniving, manipulative little witch. Not much chance you could ever fall in love with someone like that, is there?"

"Don't put words in my mouth, damn it!"

"Not much chance you could ever fall in love with any woman, I guess," Rebecca went on sadly. "I should have realized that sooner. Go back into the shadows where you belong, Kyle. Stay there in the darkness until it eats you alive. Forty or fifty years from now when you look back on a lifetime spent alone, try to remember that there was one woman who tried to pull you out into the daylight. Remember that there was one woman who truly loved you. For a while. But you couldn't love her in return."

"I told you once I gave you everything I had to give a woman."

She nodded. "And it wasn't very much, was it?"

"Damn you, Rebecca." He reached for her, his fingers tightening around her arms. "What are you trying to do to me?"

"Nothing, Kyle," she said wearily. "I'm just taking myself out of the cross fire. You and Glen do whatever you want with that land. Have your showdown at high noon right out there on Main Street in front of Cully's Tavern. I don't care who wins. The important thing is that it's now just between the two of you. The women of my family are no longer involved."

She stepped around him and walked resolutely toward the motel. It was time to leave.

"You can't walk away from me," Kyle yelled furiously. "I'm not through with you yet." But she didn't turn around. Kyle watched her go, his hands flexing into frustrated fists at his sides. "Damn you, Becky," he whispered. "You can't walk away from me. I won't let you."

The door of the café swung open. Darla stood on the threshold. She glanced at the retreating figure of Rebecca and then she looked at Kyle. Her eyes no longer held mischief, but rather a deeply contemplative expression.

"My, my," she said quietly. "Looks like the new town marshal has just made the streets safe for peaceful folk once more. And now she's going to ride off into the sunset in the best tradition of heroic western lawmen. Or should that be lawwomen? We'll all stand around wondering who she was and where she's headed next."

"This isn't a joke, Darla."

"No," she agreed. "It's not. But I think it just might be the end of a really dumb feud that's gone on far too long and involved too many innocent bystanders. Glen is waiting for you inside. I've given him my opinion on the subject of what to do with that land. Now it's up to you two."

Kyle said nothing as she came down the steps. When she was right in front of him she looked up at him and smiled.

"You know something, Kyle? I forgot to thank you."

"For what?" he asked suspiciously.

"For letting me go so easily when I broke our engagement four years ago. Oh, I know you put up a token protest. You had to, because there was a Ballard involved and therefore your ego took a bruising. And as a general principle Stockbridges never let go of anything without a serious argument. But even when you showed up at the wedding and created that awful scene, I still knew I was lucky."

"Lucky to get away from me?" He turned his head to watch Rebecca disappear behind a row of parked cars in the motel lot.

"Uh-huh. You could have made things much more difficult for me," Darla said thoughtfully. "In fact, if you had really wanted me, really loved me, I don't think I would have gotten free at all. But, who knows? Maybe if you had really loved me, I wouldn't have wanted to leave in the first place." She smiled as he looked back at her with a glowering frown. "It will be interesting to see how easily you let Rebecca go."

Kyle caught her arm as she went past him. "Whatever else happens, Rebecca isn't getting away from me. You go tell her that."

"What are you going to do?"

"I've got business to attend to." He released her, jammed his hat down over his eyes and went up the steps and back into the café.

Glen Ballard lounged in the booth, finishing off

the French fries his wife hadn't eaten. For some reason it struck Kyle as odd to see Ballard calmly eating his wife's leftover fries. It seemed like such an ordinary, mundane, husbandly thing for an enemy to do.

It occurred to Kyle that although he'd been raised in the same small community as Ballard there was a hell of a lot he didn't know about the man. Enemies tended to have a very narrow perspective on each other.

Kyle dropped into the booth across from his lifelong opponent.

Ballard grinned faintly. "This town is going to have enough gossip to last for the next ten years. Imagine a Ballard and a Stockbridge sitting down to have lunch together."

"This isn't exactly a luncheon meeting."

"We're eating, aren't we? Here comes your hamburger, now."

Kyle glanced up in annoyance as Jan set the platter in front of him. The young woman looked nervous. She removed herself immediately and skittered back toward the kitchen.

"What the hell's wrong with her?" Kyle muttered.

Glen munched another French fry. "I think she's jittery now that the women have left. As long as Darla and Rebecca are around, everyone thinks we're under control. But with the two of us sitting alone here, anything could happen. Who knows? Whole damned booth might go up in flames."

"What makes people think Darla and Rebecca can control us?" Kyle asked irritably.

"Word about our chipping in together to buy a round of drinks in Cully's and our unplanned swim last night has spread. Our reputation as big, tough, macho types is still a little damp. Darla says folks are calling Becky the new town marshal. We're the bad guys, in case you haven't noticed."

"This is crazy. Crazy and stupid. Women's games." Kyle started to shove his hamburger aside but abruptly realized he was hungry. He removed the top half of the bun and poured catsup with a liberal hand. Then he replaced the bun and took a huge bite. The taste of rare meat was vaguely reassuring.

"So," Glen said sardonically, "the way I see this, it's all your fault."

"My fault!"

"You're the one who found Rebecca first. You're the one who got her involved. You're the one who got her mad enough to come up here and set up this stupid situation. If you hadn't tried to one-up me, we wouldn't be in this mess. The lawyers would have found her. You and I could have made our offers in a straightforward, businesslike manner. She wouldn't have known anything about the history of Harmony Valley. She would have picked the offer she liked best and that would have been the end of it."

"Don't give me that bull. You were looking for

her as hard as I was. I just got lucky first, that's all."

"Lucky? I'm not sure that's the right word under the circumstances. But, then, the Stockbridge luck always has been overrated."

Kyle took another large bite of burger. "Let's skip the rehash of how we got into this and take it from there. I don't suppose you want to do the reasonable thing and let me buy you out?"

"Hell, no. This is as close as a Ballard has ever come to owning Harmony Valley. Don't expect me to walk away from my half of that land." There was a delicate pause before Glen continued smoothly. "I don't reckon you want to do the sensible thing and let me buy you out?"

"Forget it." Kyle polished off the last of his hamburger and leaned back in the seat. "Now what?"

"Beats me." Glen gave him a reflective look. "You know something? I never really thought too much about what I'd do with Harmony Valley if I ever did get hold of it. Somehow it always seemed like it would be enough just to own it finally. You got any ideas?"

Kyle stabbed a French fry into a blob of catsup. "It's occurred to me from time to time that Harmony Valley has the makings of a fine ski resort."

"A ski resort? That's the stupidest idea I've ever heard." Glen's reaction was clearly an automatic one.

"It could be done."

Glen gave that some thought. "It would take cash. A lot of it."

"Yeah."

"A successful resort would bring a lot of money into this area. Create jobs. Bring new business into the community."

"If it was done right."

Glen gazed out the window. "You see the two of us working together on something like that?"

"No." Kyle finished his fries and reached for the leftovers on Rebecca's plate. They were cold.

"Neither do I. Stockbridges and Ballards never work together. We'd draw blood every time we had to make a decision."

"It would never work," Kyle agreed.

"The alternative is to let the land sit there until my son grows up and inherits it." Glen chuckled. "Not a bad idea. If I wait long enough, Harmony Valley will eventually belong one hundred percent to Ballards, anyway."

Kyle eyed him. "What about my son?"

"I'm not real worried about him. I figure at the rate you're going, you won't be producing any heirs."

"At the rate I'm going?" Kyle prodded softly, telling himself to hang on to his temper for a few more minutes. This was, after all, business.

"The lady you just sent packing is the one female on the face of the earth who might be able to handle marrying you," Glen said. "Letting her go was a typical piece of Stockbridge idiocy. But I figure it will work to my advantage, as usual.

You're going to have a damned tough time finding another woman who will stick around long enough to give you an heir. So my boy will just naturally inherit the whole of Harmony Valley one of these days."

"An interesting scenario, but I wouldn't pin my hopes on it if I were you. I've got plans for Rebecca."

"Yeah, but is she going to go along with them? That woman's got a mind of her own."

"Let me worry about Becky," Kyle said forcefully. "We've got other things to discuss."

Glen nodded thoughtfully. "A ski resort, huh?"

"You're right. It would never work," Kyle said broodingly.

"A partnership between a Stockbridge and a Ballard wouldn't have a snowball's chance in hell."

There was silence for a long moment and then Kyle said musingly, "You remember that Halloween when the two of us went out to Alice's place and chased off those creeps who were going to trash the barn?"

Glen nodded. "I remember."

"We worked together then."

"True. For about an hour." Glen fell silent again. "I reckon we could try putting together a plan for a ski resort in Harmony Valley. Maybe if you and I stayed at arm's length, and we let our assistants do most of the work..."

"Don't kid yourself. When it comes to Harmony Valley, neither of us is going to be able to keep our hands off. This isn't going to be a routine development project."

"Maybe if we had a couple of peacekeepers around to chaperon us, we could refrain from slitting each other's throats. Darla and Rebecca might be able to manage things."

Kyle considered that. "Maybe."

Another long silence fell.

"You know," Glen finally observed, "our fathers and grandfathers must be turning over in their graves."

"I'll bet Alice and her mother are having a good laugh somewhere, too." Kyle ate the last cold French fry from Rebecca's plate and got to his feet.

Glen rose and reached for his hat. "I see Jan hovering down at the cash register with our tab. Probably too scared to bring it over to us."

"I'll take care of it."

"Like hell you will," Glen said amicably. "No Stockbridge is buying me lunch. You take care of your half, and I'll take care of mine."

"Suit yourself." Kyle grinned suddenly as he tossed a few bills down onto the counter.

"What's so funny?" Glen added an equal amount to the small pile of cash.

"You told Rebecca we couldn't even split an apple pie. And we just split the lunch check. Not bad for our first effort at doing business together."

"Don't get too excited. I expect it will be all downhill from here on in."

Kyle smiled thinly in agreement. "I expect it will. Trouble is, I don't see any other choice for us but to figure out how to put this project together."

"You ever had a feeling you've been caught in your own trap?" Glen asked reflectively.

"Yeah, I've had that feeling a lot since I met Rebecca." He walked out of the café, aware that everyone in the place was watching, open-mouthed in astonishment. A Stockbridge and a Ballard had just dined together, and neither was bleeding.

He knew the new town marshal would probably get the credit.

Kyle headed toward the motel, not bothering to give his new business partner a backward glance. He had a few things to discuss with Rebecca now that his temper had cooled.

It came as a shock when he discovered that Rebecca had checked out ten minutes earlier.

A cold shiver of dread went through Kyle. It had finally happened. He had lost his temper with Rebecca, and she had run from him just as his wife had run from him. Just as Darla had run from him.

Just as his mother had run from his father.

But there was one major difference this time around. He wasn't going to let Rebecca go the way he had let Heather and Darla go. And Kyle was damned if he would give up and sink back into himself the way Cale Stockbridge had done when Martha had fled.

Kyle vowed he would find Rebecca if he had to

track her down to the ends of the earth. She wasn't going to get away with teaching him about love and then walking out on him.

"You can run, lady," he said softly, "but you can't hide."

Ten

The next four days were the worst Kyle had ever experienced in his life. He spent them in a desperate search for Rebecca. He wasted one entire day looking for her in the mountains: Alice Cork's place, the motel, the Ballard house. He tried motels in neighboring towns. Then he got into the Porsche and drove back to Denver, anguish and anger eating at him all the way.

She had run from him. Kyle couldn't seem to absorb the shock of it. Deep inside, in spite of all the turmoil of recent days, in spite of the past, a part of him had counted on Rebecca staying with him.

Was this the way it had been for his father when Martha Stockbridge had fled? He wondered how any man could go on after a part of him had been ripped to shreds.

Kyle increased the speed of the Porsche as he left the mountains. He had to find Rebecca. He wasn't going down the same route his father had taken. He would not turn into the bitter, joyless man his father had become. Damned if history was going to repeat itself again. He was not his father, and Rebecca was sure as hell not a weak, fragile, overly delicate female who couldn't handle a man's temper.

Kyle was not going to repeat his father's mistakes. At least not every damned one of them. Not if he could help it.

He would find Rebecca and explain that to her. He would explain it very, very clearly, Kyle told himself grimly.

But by Sunday Kyle finally admitted to himself he wasn't going to locate her very easily in Denver. He had checked her old apartment, her favorite restaurants, even left messages at the major hotels. At night he prowled his condominium, pacing from room to room as if expecting her ghost to materialize.

Kyle got out of bed on Monday morning and remembered he had a business to run. He couldn't ignore Flaming Luck Enterprises any longer. He had already been away a full week without checking in. Lord only knew how Harrison was getting along with no sharp, efficient, capable executive assistant there to cover for the boss's absence.

He stood under the shower for fifteen minutes, shaved with acute precision, found a clean shirt and forced himself to eat some cereal. But none of the familiar morning rituals had the power to erase the ravages left by the events of the week.

Even Kyle could tell he looked like something

out of the bottomless pit. He took one glance in the hall mirror, saw the darkness around his eyes, the grim lines that etched his mouth and noted the fact that he badly needed a haircut. He ran his fingers roughly through his dark hair, trying to tame it. Then he gave up the effort.

He rode the elevator downstairs and climbed into the Porsche. The car's sophisticated engine howled in commiseration as Kyle sent the vehicle roaring out of the garage. On the way to the office, Kyle tried to think of where to look next for Rebecca. He could pull her personnel file and get the addresses of her relatives.

As he pulled into the lot and parked, he decided it was time to hire the same private-investigation agency that had located her in the first place.

"Good morning, Mr. Stockbridge." Theresa Aldridge looked up in surprise as Kyle stalked into the office. "We didn't know whether to expect you today or not."

"I own the place, remember?"

"Yes, sir," she said politely. "I do remember." She eyed his grim appearance and cleared her throat. "Did you have a pleasant vacation last week?"

"I had one hell of a lousy time, Theresa."

"I'm delighted to hear that, Mr. Stockbridge," Theresa said automatically. Belatedly her eyes widened. "Excuse me, I mean…"

"Never mind, Theresa. I know exactly what

you mean. What's going on around here? I see the building hasn't fallen down in my absence."

Undaunted, Theresa assumed the professional air of an executive secretary. "Most of your messages have been handled already, of course, but there are a few I held for you." She reached for a pad. "Do you want to go over them now?"

Kyle stifled an oath. "Yeah. Bring them in with my coffee."

A familiar gleam lit Theresa's eyes. "Mr. Stockbridge, you know how Miss Wade feels about secretaries getting coffee for their bosses."

"Unfortunately for you, Theresa, Miss Wade does not run this business." Kyle slammed open the door of the inner office. "At least not any longer, she doesn't," he added under his breath. Damn, what he wouldn't give to have her back, managing ways and all. He would make his own coffee every morning if it meant he could share it with Rebecca. "And what did you mean that most of my messages have been handled already?" he called out to her.

"Mr. Harrison handled some, and the rest were taken care of in the usual manner."

Kyle ignored the cryptic response and closed the door. The 'usual manner' during the past two months had come to mean that Rebecca had taken care of things.

Kyle scanned the familiar room. His office looked as neat as a pin. There were no piles of papers awaiting his attention, no memos from managers and no list of calls that had to be returned

ASAP. Kyle yanked off his jacket and stood glowering down at the clean desk. Then he leaned over and stabbed the intercom button.

"I get the feeling I'm not really needed around here, Theresa. Where the hell is all the work that must have accumulated last week?"

"The routine matters have all been taken care of, sir."

Kyle gritted his teeth as he released the intercom. Before Rebecca had taken over, no one would have dared assume responsibility for taking care of the kind of 'routine' matters that hit Kyle's desk. His staff had been thoroughly corrupted, he decided. Apparently everyone and his cousin felt free to wander into the president's office and take charge. Harrison had clearly overstepped himself.

The fact that there was something to get mad about was somehow reassuring. Kyle felt some of his inner turmoil settle as he found a focus for his tormented emotions. He would chew on someone for this. Maybe lots of someones. He'd start with Harrison.

Right after he had his coffee.

Kyle dropped into his chair. He really needed his coffee this morning. He wondered if Theresa had been so thoroughly liberated that she would feel bold enough to ignore his direct order for a cup of caffeine. Rebecca had certainly left her mark on Flaming Luck Enterprises.

Kyle punched the intercom again. "I want that cup of coffee now, Theresa. I'm not in a mood for power games this morning. Bring me a cup of coffee or start looking for another job."

There was silence for a moment from the outer office. Then Theresa's voice came back, laced with icy polish. "Your coffee is on its way, sir. Along with the weekly report you missed last Friday."

Kyle slumped back in his seat, telling himself he had to take his victories where he could get them these days. Rebecca didn't approve of terrorizing secretaries, but sadly for Theresa, Rebecca was no longer here to soothe the dragon.

Kyle was reaching for the phone book to find the number of the investigative agency he had hired two-and-a-half months ago, when his door opened. He didn't look up.

"Thanks, Theresa," he growled sarcastically.

"I thought we'd broken you of your habit of using Theresa as your personal waitress," Rebecca said calmly as she put a full mug of coffee down on the desk in front of him.

Kyle dropped the phone book. He swung around to face the apparition standing on the other side of his desk.

"*Rebecca.*"

Her eyebrows rose quizzically. "Who were you expecting? A French maid?" She waved a clipboard and slipped into the chair across from him. "I have the weekly report right here. A number of things have accumulated during the past few days. Mr. Harrison and I took care of most of the routine matters on Thursday and Friday but there are a couple of items that need your personal attention. The Jennings-Hutton deal is at risk, I think. We need to take some decisive steps on that one."

Kyle shot to his feet, his palms slapping the top of the desk. "You were right here Thursday and Friday? I've turned this town upside down looking for you."

She regarded him silently for a long moment. "Did you?"

"Becky, I've been going out of my mind trying to find you."

"I've been right here all along. Where did you think I'd go?"

He wanted to shake that too-serene, too-knowing expression off her face but he didn't dare touch her. Not yet, at any rate. If he did he would be too likely to rip her clothes off and lay her down on the couch across the room. Kyle told himself to calm down. He had to think clearly. He kept his hands on his desk, mostly to stop them from trembling.

"You ran away from me," he finally said very softly.

"I left the mountains without bothering to talk to you about my plans," Rebecca said. "But I didn't 'run away' from you. I do not run from anything. You should know me better than that by now, Kyle."

He shook his head to clear it. Part of him still believed he was hallucinating. "All I knew was that you were gone."

"I returned to work," she said, lifting one shoulder dismissively. "That's all."

"I checked your old apartment. You weren't there."

"I've been staying at a hotel while I hunt for a new apartment," she explained a little too casually.

"Is that right?" Kyle straightened. "You must have picked a very obscure one. I left messages with most of the big hotels and motels."

"Really?" she asked a bit too brightly. "Why?"

Kyle's rush of relief was beginning to fade. In its place was a sense of growing irritation. He began to realize Rebecca might be playing games with him. "Why?" he repeated carefully. "Because I was trying to locate you, of course."

"Why?" she said again.

Kyle shot her a ferocious glance and then paced over to the floor-to-ceiling window. He stood looking out at the mountains and tried to figure out what was going on. "Why the hell do you think I was looking for you, Becky?"

"I have no idea," she returned crisply. "But since you've found me, shall we go over the weekly report?"

"No, we are not going to go over the weekly report." Kyle swung around to confront her. "We are going to talk, damn it."

"About what?"

"About us. And don't give me that innocent look. You must have been listening a few minutes ago when I informed my secretary I was not in a mood for games. I meant it. I've had a rough week, Becky, and it's all your fault. You've put me through enough hoops. Give me a break, lady. I've paid for my mistake.''

She sat back in her chair, eyeing him consideringly. Kyle saw the flash of awareness in her amber gaze and he relaxed slightly. The pose of prim, polite calm was a facade. Underneath, she was as tense as he was.

"I don't think I understand," she said.

"You understand well enough. And I think I'm finally beginning to figure it out, myself. You've been twisting the knife, haven't you? Taking all the revenge you can get. It's not enough that you're forcing me to become a business partner with Glen Ballard. Oh, no, Becky Wade wants every last drop of blood. She exacts vengeance for two women she's never even met and then goes on to take some for herself. You're a greedy female. You must have known what you were doing to me when you disappeared."

Rebecca looked down at the notes on her clipboard. "That's not true, Kyle. I wasn't at all sure what my leaving would do to you. I only knew I needed time to think. I figured this was the last place you'd look for me."

"You know me so well."

"I've learned a lot lately," she admitted.

He rubbed the back of his neck. "More than I ever wanted you to know."

"You were wrong to keep things hidden from me, Kyle."

"I didn't think I had a choice." He turned back to the view of the Rockies. "I didn't know how to tell you. I didn't know how much you could take. I was afraid that if you knew it all—the fact that I'd gone to such lengths to get Harmony Valley, that I had a failed marriage and a broken engagement behind me—you'd walk away from me. What smart woman wouldn't? Then, just when I was beginning to hope you might be able to handle everything after all, you went and pulled that stunt with the land. And I finally lost my temper with you. Something I swore I'd never do."

"It was bound to happen sooner or later," Rebecca pointed out mildly.

He shook his head firmly. "No. I wasn't going to let it happen."

"A noble objective, but hardly practical. You've got the devil's own temper, Kyle, and while I know you're capable of controlling it most of the time, there are certainly going to be occasions when it gets away from you. But, frankly, I fail to see what the big fuss is all about."

He shot her a quick, searching glance over his shoulder. "I said some terrible things to you."

"You called me a sneaky, conniving, manipulative little witch," she agreed. "But under the circumstances, I'll have to admit you had some cause. I did connive to manipulate you and Ballard into working together. I hate to tell you this, Kyle, because I know how much you and everyone else enjoy the legend of the Stockbridge temper, but I'm afraid it's overrated."

Kyle planted a hand against the wall and stared at her. He must have misunderstood, she thought. "Overrated?" he finally got out.

She nodded briskly, the office lights causing her neatly bound hair to gleam. "Overrated. As dragons go, you'll do in a pinch, I suppose. After all, there is plenty of fire when you open your mouth. But you don't do all that much damage. You've got a lot more self-control than you or anyone else gives you credit for having."

For some reason that annoyed him. "Let me get this straight. You're telling me you don't find my temper very alarming?"

Rebecca grinned fleetingly. "I'll admit it can be quite stunning for short periods of time, but the impact doesn't last long. As usual, when you get to the bottom of a legend, you find out it's based on a lot of hot air."

"I think I resent that," he said, bewildered, "but I'm not sure I want to argue about it right now. If it wasn't my temper that made you disappear for four days and if you felt you had your revenge for my not telling you the truth about Harmony Valley, then just why did you leave?"

"I told you, I needed time to think."

"About us?"

"Yes."

Kyle allowed himself a flash of real hope. She was still here working for him, and she was through punishing him for the Harmony Valley fiasco. She claimed she wasn't particularly intimidated by his temper. She must still feel something for him. She *had* to feel something for him. He licked dry lips and forced himself to stay calm.

"Come to any conclusions?" he asked.

"As a matter of fact, I have."

He closed his eyes briefly, trying to read the nuances of her voice. It was impossible. He opened his eyes and met her amber gaze. "Well?"

Rebecca got to her feet, still holding the clipboard, and stood facing him. "I have decided to marry you."

If the window had been open behind him, Kyle knew he probably would have fallen through it. *"Marry me?"*

"That's right. The one thing that has been forcibly impressed on me lately is that Stockbridge males do not have what you'd call a knack for handling relationships with women. I told you the morning we went riding that the men in your family—you included—are not very good at picking out their wives. Therefore, I have decided to take the matter out of your hands. I'm making the decision for you. As you know, I'm very good at making decisions."

The world seemed to tilt around him. Kyle stared at Rebecca's composed face until things righted. "Becky, are you sure? You know what a disaster my first marriage was. Hell, the second time around, I couldn't even manage to stay engaged."

"I realize the thought of marriage makes you nervous. That's understandable, given your record. However, this time around you can relax. I'm taking charge, and there won't be any mistakes."

"You're sure of that?" he asked sardonically. But inside he was awash in a rush of euphoria. A fierce excitement raced through him, leaving him almost breathless. Kyle was afraid to move for fear of breaking the spell.

"Quite sure," she said demurely.

"When?" he demanded.

She tapped a pen against the clipboard and pursed her lips thoughtfully. "Well, there are one or two steps that must be taken before we sign the papers."

"What steps?" he asked thickly.

"I want a courtship," she told him. "A real courtship."

Kyle was dumbfounded. "A courtship," he repeated weakly.

"I want it all, Kyle. Everything I didn't get with you the first time around. Flowers, dancing, sweet talk, a ring and a big wedding. And that's not all." Her chin rose proudly. "I want you to tell me you love me."

"I love you," he said without even stopping to think. The words came with astonishing ease. They crackled in the air, and he listened to them over and over again, hearing the ring of truth. Kyle suddenly felt raw and vulnerable. "I love you so much, it's tearing me apart."

Rebecca smiled. "That's an excellent start," she said approvingly. "You may pick me up for dinner tonight at seven. I'll give you the address of the hotel where I'm staying."

"No. You'll come home with me," he told her fiercely. "I want you back under my roof. We'll go to dinner, if that's what you want, but I want you to come home."

"Not until we're married, Kyle. I told you, I want a courtship. We're going to do this my way. We already tried yours and it didn't work." She sat down again and glanced at her clipboard notes. "Now that we have that clarified, I think it's time we went over the weekly report, don't you?"

It slowly dawned on Kyle that the situation was out of control. She was going to tease him and bait him and torment him for God only knows how long before she came back to him. Rebecca Wade was running amok with power.

He took one long step forward and snatched the clipboard out of her fingers. "No, you don't, Becky," he said bluntly. "This has gone far enough. I love you, and from all indications you love me. That settles it. We'll get married as soon as we can get a license. I'm not going to let you put me through another set of hoops, lady. You've connived, manipulated and otherwise created enough havoc in my life. Be satisfied with your vengeance and let's call off the war."

She reached for her clipboard. "I want a court-ship, Kyle. Hearts and flowers. Big wedding. The works. I'm not going to move in with you until I get it."

"Becky, why?" he raged helplessly. "It's a stupid waste of time."

"I don't see it that way," she said softly. "It has become painfully apparent that the Stockbridge men need a bit of polishing."

"And you're willing to do the polishing?"

"It's the least I can do for the man I love."

Rebecca determined that Kyle would never know just how badly she had been shaking when she left his office that morning. She'd held her breath, but during the days that followed, it became clear that her gamble had paid off.

Kyle loved her, and he was willing to prove it with a courtship. Her office and hotel room were filled with flowers. She was taken dining and dancing every night of the week. The dinners were candlelit and the dancing was intimate.

But the best part was that most of the shadows that had always cloaked Kyle were receding once again. In the days that followed Rebecca's announcement of her intention to marry him, Kyle smiled and joked and laughed more than he had during the previous two months.

Over the candlelit dinners, Kyle began to open up and talk to Rebecca. About his past. About his father. About the future. It was as if he'd been freed from a time warp.

And he was insatiably curious about Rebecca, too. He wanted to know everything about her. She answered his questions, half amused, half enthralled and watched as he emerged into the full light of day.

There were times when the infamous Stockbridge temper flared briefly. Most notable was the first occasion when Rebecca had said goodnight to Kyle at her hotel-room door. He had accepted the fact that she would not come home with him, but he clearly had not been expecting her to refuse to return to the intimacy of their earlier relationship.

"Becky, this is crazy," he raged in a tight voice as he stood in the hall outside her room. "Let me in."

"No," she said gently. "Not yet."

"*I want you.* Damn it. If you close that door in my face, I'll break it down."

A door opened down the hall, and a plump, middle-aged man stuck his bald head out into the corridor. "Hey, keep it down out there. We're trying to sleep."

Kyle sent the man a look that caused him to quickly close his door.

"You're causing a scene, Kyle," Rebecca said. "I'd appreciate it if you didn't. I know Stockbridges are good at scenes, but Wades don't care for them."

Kyle swore. "Let me inside. We'll talk about this."

"No, we won't. If I let you inside, I won't be able to get you back out again."

His eyes gleamed. "I'm glad you realize that."

"Get lost, Kyle," she said with a soft laugh. "I'll see you at work in the morning."

"Becky, this hotel must be costing you a fortune. You don't need to stay here. Come back to my place. There's a spare bedroom."

"Which I'd never get a chance to use. No, thanks, Kyle." She yawned. "Excuse me. Got to get my sleep if I'm going to be any use to you in the morning."

"I've got a use for you right now," he began and then swore again, this time with resignation as the door closed gently in his face.

Rebecca leaned back against the door and listened to his footsteps as they faded away down the hall. Then she smiled to herself and began to get ready for bed.

The man loved her. There could no longer be any real doubt. She'd been almost certain all along but now she was finding out for sure. She would wait a little longer, however, before she put him out of his misery.

She shook her head ruefully as she snagged her nightgown from the closet and went toward the bathroom. It was beyond her why the Stockbridge wives and the Cork women hadn't ever figured out how to handle the Stockbridge men.

The trick was to stand up to them. After you did that, you put them on a short rein. The Stockbridges had all been strong men, and strong men needed strong women who didn't put up with too much nonsense.

Another couple of weeks of flowers and can-

dlelit dinners, Rebecca decided, and she would
tell Kyle it was time to give her the ring.

But the following Friday afternoon, Rebecca's
plans went awry. Kyle appeared in her office
shortly before five o'clock. He had changed his
clothes. He was no longer wearing the suit and tie
he'd had on all day. In their place were the familiar denims and the black Stetson. Something in
Kyle's green eyes put Rebecca on the alert. A
strange shiver of anticipation went through her.

"You have plans for the weekend?" she asked
blandly.

"Yes, ma'am, I do." Kyle smiled, showing a lot
of teeth.

Rebecca did not trust that smile. "What sort of
plans? Are you going up to the ranch?"

"Right, first time. I always did say you were
one sharp administrative assistant." He slapped
the hat against his thigh and smiled again.
"You're coming with me."

She put down the pen she had been holding
and regarded him warily. "Am I?"

"Yeah."

Rebecca thought about that. "I don't think so.
I've already explained to you that I'm not going
to spend a night with you until after we're married."

"The problem with you, lady, is that you're too
damned rigid. You need to learn to give a little
here and there." Kyle's teeth flashed.

"You think you can behave yourself for a

whole weekend? Will you let me have the spare bedroom without pestering me?"

"You can have whatever bedroom you want," he said as he came around the desk. "But whichever one you choose, you'd better expect to find me in it."

"Kyle!"

Rebecca yelped and jumped out of her chair, but there was no room to run. He caught her before she could even blink and tossed her lightly over his shoulder.

"Kyle Stockbridge, don't you dare carry me out of here like this. What will everyone think?"

"They'll think I've finally had enough of jumping through hoops. And they'll be right. Lately I've been feeling like a bull being led around by a ring in its nose. I've given you courtship, Becky. Now I'm going to take you to the mountains and make love to you until you can't think straight. I've had enough of your managing ways for a while."

He carried her out of the office, heedless of the astonished, delighted stares of his staff. When he reached the elevator, Rick Harrison held the door and then stepped in behind his boss. He was smiling broadly.

"You two have interesting plans for the weekend, I take it?" Rick asked blandly.

"We're going up into the mountains," Kyle explained, patting Rebecca's derriere. "Becky needs some fresh air and exercise."

"I see. Have a good time," Rick said as the elevator doors opened on the ground floor.

"We will," Kyle promised as Rebecca made a muffled, unintelligible comment.

He stepped out of the elevator and carried his burden outside to where his black steed was parked in the president's slot. Then he put Rebecca into the Porsche and drove away with her into the night.

ELEVEN

The night was chilled and clear, and there was virtually no traffic on the mountain road. Rebecca felt safe and snug inside the Porsche. Beside her Kyle drove with an easy control that reminded her of the way he handled his horse, Tulip.

The atmosphere in the car had been one of thoughtful serenity. Rebecca knew it was because they were both aware that the war was over. Kyle had accepted his punishment with relatively good grace but felt it had gone far enough. For her part Rebecca realized she had made her point and that it was time to end the sparring. They were two strong people who understood and accepted each other's limits.

They were in love and now, finally, that was the only thing that really mattered.

They stopped for dinner at a small café. Neither Kyle nor Rebecca said much during the meal, but the silence between them was a comfortable one.

The Flaming Luck ranch house was waiting for them, dark and alone in the night. But when they entered and started turning on lights, the shadows were dispelled.

"I think this place may have a few possibilities after all," Rebecca said as she surveyed the stark, rustic interior.

"What it needs," Kyle said as he finished building a fire and went to pour two drinks, "is a woman's touch."

Rebecca smiled lovingly up at him as she accepted her glass. Then she stood on tiptoe and brushed his mouth lightly with her own. "That's what Stockbridges in general have needed all along. They just didn't know how to pick the right women to touch them."

Kyle stood very close, looking down at her with eyes that gleamed with warmth and an aching longing. "I had the sense to pick you, didn't I?"

"I suppose we'll have to give you some credit, although you didn't seem to know what to do with me after you picked me."

"Now that is an outright slander. I knew damned well what to do with you. I made love to you as often as possible, if you'll recall."

Rebecca looked up at him. "And that's what you're going to do tonight?"

"That's what I'm going to do tonight," he vowed.

"Good. If you want to know the truth, I was getting awfully tired of that hotel room."

Kyle laughed softly. "But you were too damned proud to admit it. That's why I decided to take matters into my own hands tonight. I felt sorry for you."

"Sorry for me!"

He smiled with slow promise. "Sure. Don't you think I know what pride can do to a person? Hell, I'm an expert on the subject. You had yourself backed into a corner. I just reached over and hauled you out."

"Is that right? I've got news for you, cowboy—I was getting ready to tell you it was time to buy the ring and set the date."

"Too late, my managing little executive assistant. I've already taken care of both items." He reached into his chest pocket and took out a small package. "If you'd been in a more cooperative mood this past week, I'd have asked your opinion on the ring, at least. But since you were still having too much fun playing the lady-with-the-iron-fist-in-the-velvet-glove, I went ahead without you."

Rebecca smiled brilliantly as she opened the small box and peeked at the contents. "It's beautiful," she said simply. "Thank you, Kyle. I love it."

"Just as well, since I've scheduled the wedding for next Thursday."

Rebecca's mouth fell open. "Thursday! How in the world am I ever going to get ready by Thursday? Kyle, you can't rush something like a wedding. It takes time. We have to choose a caterer and flowers and a dress and send out invitations...mmph." The rest of her complaint was trapped behind her lips when Kyle bent down and kissed her into silence.

"Everything's been taken care of," he told her when he lifted his head.

"Who took care of it?" she demanded.

"I did. You think you're the only one capable of a little organization and efficiency?"

Rebecca was torn between outrage and laughter. She finally settled on laughter. "You're impossible." But she put down her glass and threw herself into his arms.

"I'm a man in love," he corrected as he set down his own glass and gathered her close. "That makes me capable of impossible feats."

"You've even picked out a dress?" she asked, awed.

"All by myself."

"What about the size?"

"Becky, honey, I lived with you for ten days, remember? I know your dress size. I also know your bra size and your shoe size. There is very little, in fact, that I don't know about you."

She closed her eyes, leaning her head against his chest. "And you love everything you do know?"

His arms tightened around her. "Everything. I fell in love with you on sight, you know."

"Let's not get into that," Rebecca mumbled.

He shook her gently. "It's true. I was so busy trying to juggle all the problems I'd created for myself in the process of falling for you, that I didn't stop to put a name on my emotions. But I know now that what I felt from the beginning was love. I just didn't want to admit it. I think I was afraid to admit it."

"Afraid?"

"The Stockbridge luck never holds with women," he said quietly.

She raised her head and smiled up at him. "When it comes to love, Stockbridge, you're not supposed to rely on luck."

"I think I've learned that lesson." He bent his head again and kissed her thoroughly.

Rebecca relaxed against him, savoring the warm promise of his lips. It might have been luck that had brought them together, but she knew it wasn't going to be the bond that held them. The road had been a rocky one, but at the end of it they had acknowledged what they wanted. Their commitment to each other would be unshakable.

"I love you, Becky," Kyle said hoarsely. He sank down on the sofa, pulling her down on top of him. "God, how I love you."

Sprawled on top of his hard length, her legs trapped between his, Rebecca cradled Kyle's face in her palms. "I love you," she echoed softly. "For ever and always. Nothing you could do would ever drive me away from you."

"*Becky.*" He snagged his fingers in her hair and brought her face close to his own. His mouth was tenderly ravenous, asking for complete surrender even as he silently vowed his own, unconditional capitulation.

Their clothing was discarded in slow, lingering

movements and then dropped casually over the side of the sofa. When the last of it was gone, Kyle ran his hands down Rebecca's bare back. When he reached her buttocks, he gripped her tightly. Then he lifted his thighs against hers, letting her feel the hard, aroused male flesh.

"I've been wondering," he rasped as he kissed her throat, "how you felt about kids."

Rebecca stroked the black hair back off his forehead. "I've heard Stockbridges always have sons."

"That's a fact." He kissed the hollow of her shoulder and probed gently into the warmth between her legs.

"Just like Ballards."

"The thing is," Kyle said, kissing her shoulder, "Ballard has already got a head start. But I figure if we get moving on the project, we could catch up."

Rebecca laughed softly. "I refuse to let you get me pregnant just so you can compete with Glen Ballard."

Kyle's eyes glowed with green fire. "Then how about if I get you pregnant so I can watch you get soft and round with my baby?"

Rebecca caught her breath. "You think you'd like that?"

"Lady, I'd be willing to kill for the privilege of getting you pregnant." He began to ease her legs apart.

"*Kyle.*"

"Is that a yes vote?"

"I... Oh, *yes.*"

"Let me inside," he whispered urgently, his hands guiding her until she was positioned directly above his waiting manhood. "All the way inside. I want to be a part of you again. I've been so lonely at night without you."

"Yes," Rebecca breathed again. She was trembling with the passion that flowed over her in hot waves. She touched him wonderingly, her fingers gliding through the rough hair on his chest.

"Now, baby. That's it." Kyle thrust slowly into her, at the same time pulling her down so that she took the full length of him. "*Becky.*"

She moaned softly as her body instinctively tightened around him. "I love you, Kyle."

"I know," he said thickly. "Don't ever stop, honey. I'd go off the deep end if you did. I need you so much. I love you so much."

Rebecca felt the warmth of the fire on her skin, and it seemed as though it were a caress. It supplemented the heat of Kyle's body and the flames of his passion. Her head whirled with the dizzying sensation and she lost track of everything around her, except for the strength of the man who held her.

Then she felt herself growing so tight she thought she would shatter.

"All the way, baby," Kyle urged, his own body as taut as a bowstring. "Let it go all the way. Take me with you."

She clung to him breathlessly as the glittering shards of release spun outward in a glowing spiral. Kyle was with her every step of the way, calling her name as he followed her into the mist.

And when it was over and they lay quietly together, Kyle was silent for a long while. His eyes were narrowed with contemplation as he gazed into the fire. His fingers moved lovingly in Rebecca's hair.

"It's nice to know I won't have to depend too much on the Stockbridge luck in the future," he said at last.

"What are you going to depend on?"

"You." He turned his head to look at her.

Rebecca thought she would melt all over again under the intensity of his gaze. "I'll always be here for you, Kyle." She smiled. "Even if you do slip back into your dragon ways once in a while."

"No chance of that," he assured her cheerfully. "I'm a reformed dragon."

"Sure you are. That's why you kidnapped me from the office this afternoon, right?"

He grinned. "You should have seen the expression on your face when I showed up at the door and you knew your time had run out."

Rebecca propped herself on his chest, her chin resting on her folded hands. "Actually, I thought it was kind of romantic."

"Not bad for a guy who has trouble relating to women, huh?"

"Not bad at all," Rebecca agreed. She slid her palm down Kyle's stomach to the rough thicket of hair below. When she found what she was seeking, she squeezed gently.

"Now that," said Kyle as he rolled her onto her back and came down on top of her, "is my idea of romance. Just like everyone at work always says, you have a knack for handling me."

The wedding reception was held at the Stockbridge home. In spite of Kyle's reassurances that he had taken care of everything, Rebecca found herself running around like mad during the few days available before the big event. It was hard for a born manager to let someone else manage something this important.

"Are you sure the caterers understand about the champagne?" she asked at one point.

"I'll make sure they get the word," Kyle promised easily.

"We don't want the cheap stuff. Not for all your neighbors and friends."

"Stop worrying about the Stockbridge image. It's already shot to hell, thanks to you."

"Kyle, the quality of the champagne is important."

"You have my personal guarantee we'll get the expensive stuff."

Rebecca grinned suddenly. "Something's not right here. I don't hear you screaming about the price of good champagne."

"Only the best for this wedding," Kyle vowed.

"This one's special?" she teased.

"This marriage is going to last the rest of our lives. Might as well do it right."

And so it went. But at long last she stood on the

patio, surrounded by everyone who happened to live within a radius of a hundred miles. The gown Kyle had chosen was simple and elegant in design. She felt like a queen in it. A country-western band that had a surprisingly sophisticated sound was providing plenty of lively dance music. A catering service from the nearest fair-size town had outdone itself. The array of food was staggering. Champagne flowed freely. And at the head stood a huge, tiered wedding cake.

"What do you think?" Kyle asked smugly when he managed to get close to his bride for a few minutes. "Not bad, huh?"

"I'm overwhelmed," Rebecca said honestly. "I couldn't have done any better myself. How did you manage all this on such short notice?"

"I've discovered I have a natural talent for being able to delegate," Kyle confessed.

"Aha! The truth at last. To whom did you delegate the responsibility for this wedding?"

"Never mind that now," Kyle said smoothly. He smiled possessively down at her. "Enjoying yourself, Mrs. Stockbridge?"

"I certainly am, Mr. Stockbridge." Her eyes were glowing as she looked up at him. "What about you?"

"This part's okay, I guess. But I'm looking forward to enjoying myself a lot more later on tonight. In the meantime, we'd better dance." He caught hold of her hand and led her toward the small area that had been set aside for dancing.

"Fine with me," Rebecca murmured as she

skipped to keep up with him. "But what's the rush?"

"I need to work off a little excess energy," Kyle explained as he swung her into a brisk country waltz. "It's either dance with you, or carry you inside to the bedroom and get started on the honeymoon."

Rebecca grinned, feeling the warmth deep in her body. "Think how shocked the guests would be."

"I'm not so sure about that. People around here always expect a scene from a Stockbridge." Kyle broke off, his gaze suddenly fixed on something behind her. "Or a Ballard."

Rebecca glanced over her shoulder. "Oh, good. Darla and Glen are here. I was wondering what was keeping them."

The familiar ripple of awareness went through the crowd as Glen Ballard and his wife walked into the reception.

"Don't worry. If Ballard causes a scene, I'll break his neck," Kyle promised casually, whirling Rebecca into another turn.

"Don't look so enthusiastic about the prospect. Glen is not going to cause a scene, and if you provoke one I swear I'll strangle you."

Kyle gave her an offended look. "I wouldn't provoke a brawl at my own wedding."

"Why not?" Glen said from behind him. "You did at mine. Good evening, Mrs. Stockbridge. Congratulations on finally putting a bridle on this bad-tempered brute."

"Thank you, Glen." Rebecca inclined her head politely as Kyle drew her reluctantly to a halt. "It was hard work, but I feel in the end, it was worth it. Hi, Darla. You wouldn't by any chance happen to be the one who helped Kyle get this reception organized, would you?"

Darla grinned ruefully. "How did you guess?"

"I sensed a woman's touch," Rebecca admitted.

Kyle groaned. "Thanks for ruining my image, Darla. I almost had her convinced I'd put this whole scene together through brilliant planning and executive ability."

"How could you have done it? You were running around Denver, trying to talk her into marrying you," Darla pointed out.

"I'm amazed he succeeded," Glen said. "You struck me as such a smart lady, Becky. How'd you let a guy like Stockbridge here talk you into marriage?"

"Watch your mouth, Ballard," Kyle warned equably.

"To tell you the truth," Rebecca said, "he didn't actually ask me to marry him. I had it on the agenda for next week or the week after that, but Kyle sort of took things into his own hands last Friday."

"Some things," Kyle observed with lofty male arrogance, "cannot be entrusted to an executive assistant. Sometimes the boss has to take charge. I suppose you want some of my expensive champagne, Ballard?"

"I sure as hell didn't come here to drink water."

Kyle nodded brusquely. "That's what I figured." He led the way through the crowd to the table where champagne and punch were being dispensed with lavish hands. People stood aside as the two men strode toward the table. Murmurs of astonishment and speculation could be heard.

"Absolutely incredible," Darla said with relieved satisfaction as she watched Kyle and Glen depart. "Before you arrived on the scene, I wouldn't have bet a penny that those two would ever be civil to each other. Now they're business partners, thanks to you."

"They're just a couple of hard-headed males who needed to have their heads knocked together a couple of times so they could be made to see the light of sweet reason."

"Too bad some other woman didn't realize that a couple of generations back. A lot of blood and heartache might have been saved."

"Who knows?" Rebecca said thoughtfully. "It's possible their fathers and grandfathers were every bit as ruthless and intransigent as Alice Cork and everyone else claimed they were. Maybe no one could have changed them. But Glen and Kyle are two intelligent, modern businessmen who, deep inside, know better than to perpetuate a quarrel that started three generations back. The fight wasn't theirs. It was their ancestors' battle."

"You may be right," Darla said slowly. "I guess Glen and Kyle just needed a reasonable, face-saving way out of a highly charged situation. Neither of them could back down but neither really wanted to go on battling forever."

"That's what Alice Cork said toward the end of her journal. She predicted that maybe with Glen's and Kyle's generation, the old warfare could be put to rest. She said Glen changed when he married you. He turned out not to be the womanizer his father and grandfather had been, after all. He just needed an excuse to turn into a home-and-hearth type."

"And Kyle needed a woman like you," Darla murmured. "Someone who could handle him, draw him out of the darkness and not be afraid of his temper. Someone he wouldn't have to worry about loving and losing. Someone he knew he couldn't scare half to death."

"I understand they've actually started making concrete plans for Harmony Valley," Rebecca said with satisfaction.

Darla laughed. "Would you believe it? They agreed to go with Kyle's idea of a ski resort. Glen is really excited about it. Says it will do a lot of economic good for this area. People in town are already getting enthusiastic."

"I wonder how long before they get..." Rebecca's sentence died in her throat as the crowd went eerily silent. Alarmed, she whirled toward the champagne-and-punch table.

"Oh, no," Darla groaned. "I knew it was too good to last."

Kyle's voice floated over the crowd, loud and

clear as he stood glaring at Glen. "Are you crazy? What the hell do you mean, you want to hire Duncan & Crampton for the excavation work? That outfit is fifth-rate. Look at the job they did on that mall last year. I happen to know for a fact that the developer paid an arm and a leg and still had the schedule slipped three times. We'll go with Rymont's outfit."

"We damned well will not. Rymont's on the edge of bankruptcy. We can't be sure his operation could even finish the job. Shut up, Stockbridge, and stay out of this end of things. I've had a lot more experience with this kind of development than you've had."

"Yeah? When was the last time you put in a ski resort? All you've ever done are subdivisions and a couple of Mickey Mouse office buildings. This is a whole different ball game."

"I've got the kind of connections that can pull this off, if you'll just be reasonable," Ballard shot back. He thrust out his chin in open challenge. "But I don't suppose that's possible for a Stockbridge, is it?"

"You want a dose of reason? I'll be glad to give it to you." Kyle started to shrug off his formal jacket. He was smiling with grim anticipation.

Ballard started to remove his own jacket.

"Oh, no you don't," Rebecca said, sailing through the crowd with fire in her eyes. "You two are not going to ruin my wedding with a stupid brawl."

"Glen, I will never forgive you if you don't stop

this nonsense immediately," Darla said forcefully. She was one step behind Rebecca.

"Don't worry, honey. This won't take long," Ballard stated. "Besides, Stockbridge has got this coming. Remember what he did to our wedding."

"Leave it to you, Ballard, to bring up ancient history," Kyle remarked.

"Stop it, both of you." Rebecca stepped in front of Kyle.

"Glen," Darla hissed as she got in her husband's path. "You'll have to get past me and the baby in order to get to Kyle."

"Get out of my way, Becky," Kyle urged.

"Come on, Darla. This'll just take a minute," Glen coaxed.

"Darla and I are prepared to stand here all night," Rebecca said lightly. "But I, for one, can think of other things I would much rather do with my wedding night. What about you, Kyle?" She stood on her tiptoes, put her hands on her husband's shoulders and kissed him with slow, loving thoroughness.

Kyle's bunched muscles relaxed quickly. His mouth opened for her eagerly, his tongue seeking hers. Then his arms went around her waist. "Oh, yeah, baby," he growled, "I can think of plenty of other things to do tonight besides beating Ballard into the pavement. What do you say we go do them?"

The crowd roared its approval.

Behind Rebecca, Ballard sighed loudly. "Something tells me you're not going to be nearly as much fun as you used to be, Stockbridge. You've changed."

Kyle raised his head to look at his old enemy. Ballard was grinning at him, his arm around a smiling Darla.

"I got lucky," Kyle said.

Epilogue

Nine months later the Stockbridge heir arrived with a lusty squall that heralded a familiar temper. The temper wasn't the only thing that had been passed down to another generation. The baby also had Kyle's green eyes.

They named her Anna Melinda.

"I don't believe it," Glen Ballard announced when he and Darla came by the Stockbridge home to view the newest member of the family. "It's a girl. After all these years, the Stockbridges finally got smart and started having girls."

Kyle held his new daughter proudly. His grin was as wide as the Colorado skies. "Damned right," he said. "And I'll tell you something else, Ballard. This little girl of mine is going to run circles around that boy of yours."

Glen laughed. "You may be right for once. No Ballard has ever had to deal with a female Stockbridge. Should be interesting to see what happens."

Darla glanced down at the lively baby boy she

was holding on her lap. Little Justin Ballard was just starting to show evidence of his father's coppery hair. "Look at how interested he is in Anna. He can't take his eyes off her."

"That could be an omen for the future," Rebecca murmured as she poured coffee. "There was something in Alice Cork's journal about the Stockbridges and the Ballards becoming related one day through marriage. She thought it would be the perfect ending for the feud."

"Not a chance," Kyle said automatically.

"No way," Glen echoed confidently.

Rebecca grinned at Darla who smiled back knowingly.

Baby Justin ignored the adults, his gaze still fixed in utter fascination on the infant in Kyle's arms. Anna Melinda gurgled contentedly.

Kyle glanced down at his beautiful little daughter and could have sworn she winked one tiny green eye.

Take 3 of "The Best of the Best™" Novels FREE
Plus get a FREE surprise gift!

Special Limited-time Offer

Mail to The Best of the Best™

3010 Walden Avenue
P.O. Box 1867
Buffalo, N.Y. 14240-1867

YES! Please send me 3 free novels and my free surprise gift. Then send me 3 of "The Best of the Best™" novels each month. I'll receive the best books by the world's hottest romance authors. Bill me at the low price of $4.24 each plus 25¢ delivery per book and applicable sales tax, if any.* That's the complete price and a savings of over 20% off the cover prices—quite a bargain! I understand that accepting the books and gift places me under no obligation ever to buy any books. I can always return a shipment and cancel at any time. Even if I never buy another book, the 3 free books and the surprise gift are mine to keep forever.

183 MEN CF23

Name	(PLEASE PRINT)
Address	Apt. No.
City	State	Zip

This offer is limited to one order per household and not valid to current subscribers.
*Terms and prices are subject to change without notice. Sales tax applicable in N.Y.
All orders subject to approval.

UBOB-197

©1996 MIRA BOOKS

This April
DEBBIE MACOMBER

takes readers to the Big Sky and beyond...

MONTANA

At her grandfather's request, Molly packs up her kids and returns to his ranch in Sweetgrass, Montana.

But when she arrives, she finds a stranger, Sam Dakota, working there. Molly has questions: What exactly is he doing there? Why doesn't the sheriff trust him? Just *who* is Sam Dakota? These questions become all the more critical when her grandfather tries to push them into marriage....

Moving to the state of Montana is one thing; entering the state of matrimony is quite another!

Available in April 1998 wherever books are sold.

MIRA

MDM434

She's a woman without a future
because of her past.

THE DAUGHTER

At fifteen, Maggie is convicted of her mother's
murder. Seven years later she escapes from
prison to prove her innocence.

After many years on the run, Maggie makes a
dangerous decision: to trust Sean McLeod, the cop she
has fallen in love with. She knows he can do one of two
things: he can turn her in or help her find her mother's
real killer. She feels her future is worth the risk....

JASMINE CRESSWELL

Available in April 1998 at your favorite retail outlet.

MIRA

MJC425

Other titles available by

JAYNE ANN KRENTZ

Get more romance and adventure as written
by one of MIRA's most talented authors: